Contents

THE P**E IN THE JAM TART
BY
K.L. Smith

For my amazing step-son Tom and
his wonderful wife Sophia

Prologue

I panicked a little as the patronising therapist peered at me from under her purple Reg Holdsworth spectacles anxiously. I had been far too busy trying not to stare at the black hair sticking out from the mole on her forehead to have been paying much attention to what she was saying. Despite my best efforts I felt my eyes drift back to the offending black hair – not unlike a pube -and shuddered as an unwelcome memory invaded my brain.

"Claire!" She chided. "I asked you why you think you're here today. In your own words please."

I shuffled uncomfortably in my chair. "Because I was sectioned?" Didn't she know? Hadn't she read my notes?

She looked upwards, a little exasperated with me I think. "I'm aware of *why* you're here, but what I'd like to know is the circumstances that *led* to you being sectioned."

I huffed inwardly, it might be what she *meant* but it definitely wasn't what she *said*. I fiddled with my thumbs while trying to think of an answer that might appease her. The truth was, it was a long story and some of the things that I did leading up to 'the incident' baffled even me.

She leaned forward in her seat blasting me with breath that could cut glass. "Claire, if you want to get well, you have to start opening up to me. Start at the beginning and tell me as much as you can."

I was uncomfortable but decided the fastest way out of this place would be to start talking...so I began.

"I suppose it all really started one rainy Tuesday evening..."

Chapter One

I fought my way through the puddles that used to be my garden path and up to my front door, hearing rock music belting out as soon as I got within a few feet of the threshold. I wished for the umpteenth time that my son Paul would use the bloody head phones I bought him if he was going to play music that loud. My neighbours that are joined onto us are terrible for complaining about noise. Only to me though. I'm the quiet one in the family yet I'm always the one that gets the ear-bashing for noise.

Putting my key into the latch I braced my eardrums for the onslaught as the door opened. Jesus! I ran straight upstairs and marched into the little sod's bedroom and crossed the room to the stereo, where I pressed 'OFF'. What I *wasn't* expecting when I turned around, was my son with his pants around his ankles trying to hide his 'modesty' behind his laptop.

"GOD!" I turned away in horror.

"Can't you knock?" The little sod fumed.

I kept my eyes shielded as I left the room. "You wouldn't have heard me with that bloody racket!"

I left shame faced and went back downstairs to recover from my trauma.

I stepped over TLS's (The Little Sod's) school gear that he had dumped everywhere after getting home from school. His wet coat was flung over the sofa, drenching the upholstery below it. In despair I followed his muddy shoe prints across the living room carpet and into the kitchen where I found them in a muddy heap in the middle of the floor. The fridge door was still wide open with the milk bottle hanging out of the door, and there were breadcrumbs and butter streaks all over the surfaces that I had cleaned before I went to work that morning.

With a sigh I straightened the milk bottle properly and shut the fridge door before sitting down at the kitchen table and staring at the chaos around me. I put my head in my hands as I heard 'My Chemical Romance' start screaming at me from the speakers upstairs.

"What the hell have I ever done to deserve this?" I whispered at the ceiling.

I sat there for a few moments, just trying to breathe through the suppressed rage that was forever at the forefront of my brain.

Once I felt sufficiently calm and under control, I went over to the pantry and retrieved my noise cancelling headphones that a workman had left behind the previous year. I slid them over my ears and instantly the quiet enveloped me like a comforting blanket. I sighed in relief, my ear drums ringing with blessed silence. Nothing on earth could have made me go back up to TLS's bedroom to make him turn the music down after realising what he was doing in there.

Picking up my bottle of spray bleach, I started the never ending task of cleaning up after him. It was just a shame I couldn't bleach the last ten minutes from my brain.

By the time I had the kitchen back in some semblance of order I was bone weary. I'd had a hard day and was certainly not in the mood for my husband Max and his bullshit. He came in through the back door, trailing mud across my freshly mopped floor.

"Haven't you started tea yet? I'm starving." He said, jumping straight in with the demands, oblivious to the dirt he had tracked in all over my nice clean floor.

"What?"

"Take those stupid headphones off." He mimed at me.

I obliged reluctantly.

"I said, why haven't you started tea yet? I'm famished."

I bit my lip with annoyance. "I haven't had time. I've been run off my feet all day, I'll start it in a minute."

He sneered sarcastically. "What playing around in a bakery with cream cakes all day tired you out? You should try having a proper job like me, then you'd know what it means to be tired." He turned his back to me and started rummaging through the fridge.

He had a nerve criticising my job. All he did for a living was sit on his backside all day chatting on the phone to 'clients' and playing hide the stapler with his secretary in the stationary cupboard.

To keep the peace, I humoured him a little. "Was it hard work today? You said you were working late."

He raised his eyebrows slightly when he lied in reply. "What? Oh, yeah. Had inventory to do."

He then stuck his lying face back into the fridge. For a split-second I had the urge to slam the door and trap his face in there -between the door and the gone off orange juice I kept forgetting to throw out. But no, I bit my lip and got on with peeling potatoes.

It wasn't long before TLS came trudging down the stairs, nose in the air inhaling the delicious smell of the chicken I was roasting in the oven.

"God I'm starving!"

He was always starving.

"It's nearly ready." I replied, pans and lids flying around me as I worked like a whirlwind dishing up the food. How he could look me in the eye after what I caught him doing earlier I don't know. I would certainly be avoiding eye contact at all costs.

After ten seconds he whined again. "I thought you said it was nearly ready."

"It'll just be a minute. Just give me a minute would you?"

He kicked the cupboard with contempt. "God you old people are so slow!"

"Old? I'm thirty-five!"

Old! I was wounded! I found myself trying to straighten out the frown lines from my face as I carried on cooking. I was trying to make my face a blank-canvas - free of expression or lines, but I only succeeded in making Max jump when he asked me the time and my blank expression 'freaked him out.'

By the time the two irritating men in my life were fed, I turned to my own dinner, but found I had lost my appetite. It had been too long a day and I was just too tired. I pushed my plate away with a yawn.

Once the washing up was finally done I thought I'd have a soak in the bath and then get in bed and have an early night, but no. Max decided to get in the shower before I had a chance to claim the hot water from the immersion heater and by the time he'd finished twenty minutes later, all the hot water was gone. Shit! Oh well, I thought, straight to bed for an early night then?

No.

"Mum, don't forget I need my football kit washing for tomorrow morning." TLS barked before slamming his bedroom door behind him.

I groaned in horror. "You need it washing for tomorrow? Why the hell didn't you tell me earlier?"

"Ugh!" Was the reply from the closed bedroom door, before it reopened with a pile of stinking clothes flying at my face.

"Great! Just bloody great!"

I picked up the pile of sweaty stinky clothes off the floor and headed back to the kitchen with them. The washer took two hours to do a full wash cycle, then the dryer would have to be loaded. Plus, I'd have to stick around to turn the dryer off when it finished its cycle or it would keep beeping all night and drive me up the wall. At this rate I wouldn't get to bed before 2am.

So much for an early night!

***

So after a night of zero sleep, the next day started exactly the same. Demands, demands, demands. I ironed shirts, located school shoes, and did geography homework so my son wouldn't look stupid. Then it was onto cooking breakfast for them both which was met with a grunt. How many other people wake up every morning to a full English breakfast? And what do I get as thanks for my efforts? "Ugh." Ugh? Really? Ugh is the best they can do?

I stared at the pair of them grunting and dribbling their way through their breakfasts, troughing like a pair of pigs, egg yolk and bean juice dripping down Paul's school shirt that I had only just finished ironing. I could feel my right eye starting to twitch involuntarily. Max was slyly texting his mistress with his right hand as he was eating a sausage with his left hand. I walked behind him and caught sight of the text.

...**got a sausage in my hand with your name o...**

That was as much as I read before the twitch in my eye started to feel like an oncoming aneurism. My nose started to twitch and I was getting a muscle spasm in my left leg.

I took a deep breath and sat down. I would not make a scene. I would sit here, calmly irritated until they had both gone, and then I would furiously vacuum until I felt better. I would completely ignore the rage in my belly, and do a nice crossword before I went to work.

Unfortunately, this plan didn't quite work out.

Once Max had finished texting his private's investigator, he turned to me with annoyance.

"Why aren't you eating?"

"I'm not hungry." I said through gritted teeth.

"You should eat something. Breakfast is the most important meal of the day."

I poured myself a cup of tea, ignoring him.

"Have something. Anything. Even if it's just a

biscuit."

"I'm not hungry."

"Goddam it Claire have a bit of toast or something. People keep telling me you're losing weight as if it's my fault!"

God what was his problem?

"Fine." I stood up and went over to the cupboard. "I'll have a jam tart with my cup of tea or something."- And that's the moment when the shit hit the fan.

I pulled the open packet down off the shelf before recoiling in horror at the revolting sight before my eyes. There, in the centre of the last remaining jam tart, was a large black pubic hair - and it was not one of mine. I'm a natural blonde if you know what I mean. Max kept his 'garden' tidy for his secretary. So after a process of elimination, that left one person in the house with unruly black pubic hair.

I turned to the little sod in disgust. He was still shovelling beans into his mouth with a gormless expression on his face. The twitch in my eye had now turned into a full blown wink. I was winking and blinking my fury at the pair of them. Speechless! The faster my eye winked at them, the faster my left leg twitched. I blinked and twitched from one bastard to the other, winking at one, blinking at the other.

"What the hell's wrong with you?" Max looked at me oddly.

What the hell was wrong with me?

WHAT THE HELL WAS WRONG WITH ME????

That was it. The switch in my head flicked from *mild* to *homicide.* I let rip.

"THERE IS A PUBE IN MY JAM TART!!!"

They responded with a jaw drop.

"WHAT IS WRONG WITH ME? WHAT IS WRONG WITH YOU?" I turned to my bewildered husband who has never in seventeen years of marriage heard me raise my voice, and roared at him.

"YOU! Yes, YOU! You think I don't know about you humping your secretary? Well I do! You're a dirty lying man whore." As an after-thought I yelled. "AND I HOPE YOU GET CRABS!"

Then it was Paul's turn. "And YOU, you dirty little pervert, you left a pube in my jam tart! My jam tart! My jam tart has a pube in it! What the hell is wrong with you?"

I stared through my twitching eye at their bewildered faces. Both still with knives and forks in hand. I placed the offending jam tart on the breakfast table for them both to view with shame before washing my hands thoroughly. I eyeballed them both before barking. "I am going to work."

I then slammed the door as hard as I could on the way out.

Chapter Two

The therapist looked a little taken-a-back by my recount of breakfast with a pube. I could almost see her brain stuttering as she was trying to process the scene I had described. I cleared my throat a little wondering if I should disturb her. Finally, with a shudder she asked…

"Is this the first time you've lost your temper with your family?"

I shrugged. "It was the first time I lost my temper with anyone really. I don't like confrontation."

The therapist peered at me with one raised eyebrow (caterpillar). "So how do you deal with day-to-day things normally? What happens if something or someone upsets you?"

"Nothing, I just ignore things until they go away."

She shook her head with a smirk. "And how is that working out for you?"

"Fine thank you." I said without irony.

She didn't look impressed. "So continue then, what happened after the 'pube incident'?"

***

"I was just getting on the bus as I happened to look down and saw that I still had my novelty Shaun the sheep slippers on. Good God, I thought, could the day get any worse, really?

I saw a couple of teenage boys sniggering and pointing as I made my way down the aisle to my seat.

"Yeah? What of it?" I bellowed.

They looked away quickly. Satisfied that they were no longer staring, I sat down. I looked down at my slippers in disgust. It was all the pube's fault. If not for that pube I would have been sitting here in my nice plain uncomfortable shoes, ready for work without looking like an imbecile. God knows what my bloody boss Irene will say when she sees what's on my feet. She already hates me.

I got off the bus and made my way down the street to the shop, dodging around the puddles so as not to get my stupid slippers wet. I was early so I had to knock on the door before Irene saw me and came over to let me in. She looked down at my feet bewildered.

"What the hell have you got on your feet?"

"I'm sorry. I've had a difficult morning." I couldn't possibly describe to her the devastation of finding a pube in a jam tart.

"You can't work in those. What were you thinking?"

Whoops, my eye was starting to twitch again. I better reign it in before the shouting started again.

I wasn't accustomed to shouting, in fact I had given myself a headache with it earlier.

"What should I do?" I asked.

She sighed heavily. "I'll get you my spare pair, see if they fit. What's wrong with your eye?"

"Nothing, why?"

"It's twitching."

"Probably got something in it." I lied, wiping the offending thing with a hanky from out of my apron pocket. She didn't look convinced, but she went off to find me some shoes.

They were a size too small, but I managed to jam the awful things on. I'd have a blister by the end of the day, but at least I didn't look like a simpleton.

"Right Claire, make yourself useful and start mopping that floor down."

With a sigh I picked up the mop and bucket out of the storage cupboard and made a start.

By dinnertime my borrowed shoes were crippling me. I winced every time I was forced to walk up and down the shop floor. Once I was finally allowed a dinner break I shot into the back room to put my slippers back on. Oh the relief as I took those awful shoes off. Fortunately for me, this was also the time that Jean -the homeless woman came in. For once Irene would have to serve her instead of forcing me to. Poor old Jean thinks that Irene gives her the leftovers and out-of-date stock from the day before out of the goodness of her own heart. But it's rubbish! I discretely settle Jean's bill out of my wages each week. I had a friend who used to emotionally blackmail me into supporting her many charities, everything from cancer research to support wheels for quadriplegic tortoises. Eventually I got tired of her making me feel bad for not being able to support all of her causes, and so I decided to start a sort of charity of my own. Feeding Jean. She had no idea, and I was glad. I was sick to death of people gloating about how good and charitable they were. To me, true charity doesn't need a pat on the back for it. I'm happy to help, I don't want or need credit for it.

I could see Irene grimacing from here at the smell that filled the shop every time Jean came in. She couldn't help it; doorways that come with onsuite facilities usually consist of peeing into the corner, and sticking your head outside for a shower when it's raining.

I was just putting the kettle on when Irene shouted through at me to re-stock the jam tarts and lemon curds.

"It's my dinner hour. Can I just have five minutes to have a breather first?" God that woman has a nerve, I thought rubbing my sore heel.

"I need them now! Get your bum moving or get the sack. Choice is yours!"

Putting my cup back down with annoyance, I went to pick up the tray of jam tarts when I found that I just couldn't do it. Every time I went to pick them up, I had a flash back to the contents of my own jam tart earlier.

The tick started to return to my eye, as Irene came back in barking at me. "What the hell's keeping you? I'm not paying you to dawdle!"

I turned to her, slightly paling. "I can't pick them up."

"What do you mean you can't pick them up? Has your back gone?" She eyed me, puzzled.

I shook my head.

She picked the tray up with annoyance. "Well? What is it?"

My voice came out a little shaky. "It's the pube."

"The what?"

"The pube in the jam tart."

She dropped the tray in horror. "Oh my God!"

The tray clattered to the floor with a deafening crash! Jam tarts scattered across the floor in every direction. Irene looked at me in horror. "Seriously? A pube?"

I nodded.

"Please tell me it wasn't yours!"

That brought me out of my dazed state. "It was NOT mine."

"Well who the hells was it?"

"TLS."

"What?"

"The little sod."

"What are you talking about? What little

sod?"

"My son, Paul."

She stood over me, hands on her huge hips. "Let me get this right. Your son put a pube in the jam tarts?"

"Yes."

She looked at me in disgust. "That's it. Pack your stuff and get out. You're fired."

***

I left the bakery with a heavy heart. I hadn't meant to mislead Irene about the pube, I just could not look at a jam tart without feeling sick. I certainly never meant to lose my job.

I trudged down the street in my Shaun the Sheep slippers, rudderless. What now?
I had left the house that morning without picking up my door keys. No one would be in at home until later on. What do I do now? Where do I go? Not my mother's that was for damn sure. I sat on a bench next to the bus stop while I decided what to do for the rest of the day. One thing was for certain, I couldn't trudge about all day in my slippers. I was getting too many funny looks. I supposed that I could get the bus into town and go get some shoes. I was already at the bus stop anyway, and it was only a hundred yards or so from the bus station in town to the nearest shoe shop. Yes. That sounded like a plan to me.

I stuck my arm out and flagged the first bus

down displaying 'Station' as its destination.

I clambered up the steps and paid the driver who observed. "They look comfy love." Staring down at my feet with amusement.

I put my head down ashamed. "Thanks."

I quickly made my way up the aisle to sit down when I heard someone call. "Coo-ee."

I turned in surprise to see the old lady I often share the bus with.

"Oh hello."

"I thought it was you." She patted the seat next to her. "There's room for a little one here."

I smiled and sat down at the side of her.

"How nice to see you again." She looked down at my slippers. "Should I ask?"

"It's a long story."

"Oh dear, like that is it?"

"You could say that. I just got the sack. And, to add insult to injury, I forgot my door key this morning, so I'm stuck out in my slippers until to-night when someone will be home to let me in."

"Goodness, you poor thing!"

"Thank you." I appreciated her caring manner. My hurt feelings were desperately in need of a little kindness.

"Why don't you come home with me and have a pot of tea. That'll pass the time for you a little won't it?"

"That's very kind of you, but I wouldn't want to impose. You don't even know my name; I could be a robber or a murderer for all you know."

She smiled. "I've never heard of the police scouring a crime scene for prints of Shaun the Sheep slippers."

"Touché." I smiled. "My name's Claire, by the way."

"Violet." She returned.

"Are you sure about inviting me back to your house? I wouldn't want to inconvenience you."

"I'll be glad of the company love. It'll make a nice change. I don't often get visitors these days."

I smiled my thanks in return.

She peered down at my feet again. "What size are you?"

"A six."

"In that case I can help. My daughter was a six, I've got a few pairs of her shoes kicking around."

"You still have her shoes? After all these years?"

She smiled wistfully. "You find that parents who lose children keep everything they possibly can."

I mentally chided myself. "I'm sorry I didn't know you lost a child."

"Oh that's okay love, no offense taken. I suppose one of these days I'll have to make a start clearing her room out."

I felt a little awkward. I wasn't sure what to say. I've always been awkward with people who are upset. Funerals terrify me. What the hell can you say to people in the midst of devastation? Sorry for your loss? That's too generic. Panic at the thought of saying the wrong thing normally results in me hiding when the grieving person comes near me. I know it's cowardly but I'd rather say nothing than run the risk of saying something insensitive.

Violet must have noticed my silence, as she interrupted it. "So why did you get the sack then, if you don't mind me asking?"

I looked at her kindly face. Screwed up my face in disgust and confessed to the events of the day.

She sat back in her seat stunned at my revelation of the jam tart incident. "Well I wasn't quite expecting that my dear."

I put my face in my hands with embarrassment. "You did ask." I muffled out from between my fingers.

She patted my arm gently. "These things happen." She dropped her voice. "I never thought I would actually repeat this to anyone, but given the circumstances....oh heck why not. It might make you feel a little better." She paused. "The little boy who lives next door to me built me a lovely snowman in my front garden last winter. I love snowmen and I was delighted at the charming job he made of it. After he'd gone, I put the finishing touches on it, you know, carrot for a nose, coal for the buttons....However, when I got up the next morning and opened my bedroom curtains, the snowman had been 'modified' by the little boy's older brother."

"What do you mean, 'modified'?"

She looked uncomfortable. "Well, he'd taken a second carrot, and placed it as a…a…penis, and he'd used two lumps of coal for the…you know," she mouthed the word, "testicles."

I sniggered despite trying not to. "Sorry." I said putting a hand over my mouth to try and stifle the giggle.

She smiled and shook her head. "You haven't heard the worst bit yet."

"Why what else did he do?"

She sighed heavily. "He covered the end of the carrot in mayonnaise, which I only discovered when I let my dog out. It gave me quite a turn to see my dog washing the mayonnaise off of it I can tell you."

I put my hands over my mouth to stifle the laugh that almost burst out.

She was the first to start laughing despite trying to look disdainful. Before long I gave up trying to hold it in and gave a proper belly laugh too.

I wiped a tear away from the corner of my eye and noticed some of the other passengers giving us a funny look. "Well Violet I don't feel too bad now after that."

"Good, glad to help. My late husband had rather an appropriate saying, 'When life bites you on the bottom, trump!'"

I smiled. "Words to live by Violet."

***

I followed Violet off the bus and trotted happily at the side of her making small talk along the way to her home. I was stunned as she turned into the driveway of a large old red bricked Edwardian house. I followed after her up the gravel driveway wincing as the stones found their way inside my slippers. I looked up at the house in awe, it had been my dream since I was a little girl to live in a house like this. It towered above me, three stories high, ending in gabled attic windows. Leaded windows dazzled in the midday sun, sparkling like fresh cut diamonds. These were proper lead light windows, not the plastic rubbish that I had at home. Rambling roses curled around the stone portico, blooming pink and red amidst the thorns.

I had to ask. "This is your house?"

She smiled. "Do you like it?"

"I love it."

"Well come in then. Can't have you standing about outside making the place look untidy."

I followed her over the tulip decorative tiled floor of the porch and in through the front door.

"Go through to the sitting room dear while I make the tea."

I obliged and went in through the double oak doors, marvelling at the craftsmanship of the mouldings. I sat down on an over-stuffed 1920's sofa and made myself comfortable. I looked about me in delight at the grand room. Over to one corner was a walnut baby grand piano covered in family photographs. I wandered over for a closer look. I picked up the first silver frame that contained a black and white photograph of a young couple - whom I presumed must be Violet and her husband who had his arms around her waist. Holding on to her mother's hand was a pretty child who I took to be her daughter. I was startled as Violet came in behind me with the tea things.

"Memories of happier times." she said wistfully placing the tea tray down on the maple coffee table.

"Sorry I didn't mean to be nosey."

"Not at all. It's nice to have someone to talk to. I rarely get visitors these days. Occasionally some niece or nephew calls by to see if I'm still alive. Do you take sugar dear?" She asked pouring the tea from a china tea pot.

"No thanks." I didn't know what to say about her family checking to see if she was dead yet.

"Tell me about your son." She said changing the subject to my immense relief.

"Paul? Oh he's okay really. Though he's at *that* age. Loud music, stupid haircuts, major attitude problem and now he's got an irritating girlfriend too on top of all that."

"How bad is his hair cut?" She asked with twinkling eyes.

I rolled my eyes to the heavens. "He has horns!"

"Clip on?"

"Nope, permanent. I sent him to the hairdressers last week to have his usual short back and sides, because his hair had gotten ridiculously long. But, when he got there he'd changed his mind after seeing someone in there having horns cut into their hair, so that's what he came home with, horns."

"I don't understand what you mean by horns? A pattern shaved into his hair?"

I shook my head. "No, all of his hair shaved off except for two tufts that have been left long which he hairsprays into horns!"

"Goodness me." She clutched her beaded necklace in shock.

"He's a delight." I said dryly.

"How old is he?"

"Fifteen, almost sixteen."

"Perhaps it's a phase." She said dismissively. "He'll probably grow up to be a boring accountant with a sensible haircut and shiny shoes."

"What I wouldn't give for that to be true." I shook my head. "Just as long as he doesn't grow up to be like his father."

"Why what's wrong with his father?" She asked offering me a plate of biscuits.

"He's a prat."

"Oh."

"Sorry." I paused. "No actually I'm *not* sorry, he *is* a prat. He's having an affair with his secretary."

"Oh dear I'm very sorry. Has it been going on for

long?"

"About a year I think. The worst part is though, that I'm not sure that I even care. That's awful isn't it? I should be livid, angry, jealous, but I'm not. I live in fear that he might actually confess to everything and then have to face up to, you know, divorce or something."

She was looking at me oddly. I looked away. This was why I usually kept my thoughts to myself.

She sat down next to me and said kindly, "There's no shame in not wanting to rock the boat. People are strange creatures of habit sometimes. The fear of the unknown can be terrifying."

"That's it exactly!" I cried. "The fear of the unknown. It's not that I want to spend the rest of my life with Max; it's just that I can't imagine what life would be like without him, we've been together since school."

She patted my arm. "You can't live your life in fear of the unknown. Life is a big adventure; you truly never know what's around the corner. You have to seize the day and grab every ounce of life that you can. You only get one go at it and you have to make it count."

"What if I'm too scared?" I asked meekly.

"It's okay to scared lovey, be scared if you want but don't ever let it hold you back. You can be scared to jump into a pool can't you? But you can always close your eyes and then jump anyway."

I smiled at her; she was just what I needed

today. "Thank you."

"No problem. Anytime you want someone to talk to, you come and see me. You know where I live now, I'm always here on an afternoon if you want a chat."

"You're an angel Violet."

"I'd rather be a devil." She said with a twinkle in her eye.

Chapter Three

I hurried off to the supermarket after receiving a short phone call from Max. There had been a work problem or something and there was to be an emergency meeting at our house for him and his co-workers. He wanted me to dash out to Tesco and buy some nibbles or something for the meeting. It seemed as though he had completely forgotten my outburst earlier and my declaration that I was well aware of his affair with his secretary. I just hoped I wouldn't lose my temper with her in front of everyone if she was at my house tonight. I wasn't used to having a temper, and I wasn't at all sure how to control my new power.

I forgot to mention to Max while I was on the phone about my lack of footwear. Violet had been true to her word and dug out a pair of her daughter's shoes for me -but sadly they were so old they were dropping apart at the seams.

Dropping off the bus a stop early, I waddled into Tesco ignoring the stares I was getting. After filling my stupid trolley (with the wonky wheel) with an assortment of junk food that hopefully Max would approve of, I headed home. I hoped I'd have time to clean the toilet before his dollop of trollop got there. She might be humping my husband, but I'd be damned before I'd let her see the state of the toilet rim after TLS had been using it.

Balls, I thought as I opened the front door and went inside. By the sight of the dozens of coats hung up on the coat rack, his co-workers were already here. I peered through and saw Max was seated on a kitchen chair that he'd taken into the lounge, his two other co-workers Stan and Tony were squashed up together on one the sofa, while Stephanie who worked in telesales was sharing the other sofa with Max's 'pencil sharpener' Lola. I tried not to stare at my new nemesis who was looking down at my slippers with a sneer as I came in.

All eyes turned to stare at me, well apart from Stephanie the telesales girl who had a lazy eye. One eye glared at me while the other eye was looking at my left nipple.

Max cleared his throat with annoyance at me and gestured for me to follow him into the kitchen.

Lola continued looking me up and down with a smirk as I walked passed her. I felt that little tick starting to flutter in my left eye again.

"What's going on?" I asked Max once we were out of earshot of the others. He looked visibly nervous; he had sweat patches under each arm. He obviously wasn't nervous about my being in the same room as his mistress though -judging by the wink he gave her, maybe he thought he had too many witnesses for me to make a scene? (I hated it that he knew me so well). So I was quite puzzled what had him so rattled.

He stammered. "I think I might be getting sued for discrimination."

I was a little taken aback. I would have thought if he was going to be sued for anything it would be sexual harassment. "Why what have you done?"

"Nothing!" He hissed looking back over his shoulder. "Well less than nothing, I failed to hire a racist."

I frowned in confusion. "So why are you being sued?"

"It's...complicated. I've arranged this meeting with a few colleagues to try and discuss a way forward with the situation. Can you make some tea and coffee and hand out a few nibbles or something before we get started?"

"Course." This was interesting. Max was a sexist pig of that I had no doubt, but racist? Never.

I boiled the kettle and put a few nibbles in bowls before carefully taking everything through to the lounge on a tray. As I was handing out cups of tea and coffee I was suddenly struck by the realisation that only a handful of his colleagues were here. At first I had thought that probably only a few of them could make the emergency meeting, but after Max's whispered conversation in the kitchen I realised that he had been strategic in his invitations. I handed out a cup of tea to Tony who was black, a coffee to Stan who was half Pakistani, and orange juice for Stephanie who was a white lesbian. Lola who was the Spanish tart got a drink of water that came from out of the fish tank.

"This isn't tap water is it?" She asked me snottily, flicking her long black hair over her shoulder.

"No." I answered shaking my head truthfully.

I sat down looking around at the many different faces in my lounge feeling like an extra in an anti-discrimination poster. Maybe Max was a racist? He certainly seemed to be trying to compensate for something.

Max stood up wiping his sweaty hands on his trousers and cleared his throat nervously. "Okay, well firstly, thank you all for coming and giving up your evening. This is a bit of a delicate matter, and I'd really like all of your help and input with this matter. Cards on the table? I'm completely out of my depth, and I'm hoping for as many diverse opinions as possible. Last week I received a job application from a man called Carl who seemed the perfect candidate for the job; he had experience, more than enough qualifications, lives locally and was willing to start straight away. I told him over the phone that the job was as good as his but asked him to come in for an official interview the day after." He paused pinching his nose trying to compose his thoughts. "But when he turned up I had to tell him that I couldn't hire him. He was too....different."

"In what way...different?" Asked Stephanie with

a little contempt.

"Was he too ethnic?" Stan asked narrowing his eyes.

"Gay?" Tony asked.

Max was looking decidedly uncomfortable. "He was….wearing a dress."

I laughed before I could help it. He glared at me, so I bit my lip.

Stephanie questioned him again. "So was he a transvestite?"

"No."

"Trans-gender?" She tried again.

"Partly." He conceded.

Bloody hell this was like give us a clue.

Stephanie was losing all patience with him. "So what then?"

"He says he is trapped in the wrong body. Although he says his name is Carl on his birth certificate, he wishes to be called Carly and work amongst us as a woman."

"So he *is* trans-gender then." Stephanie said triumphantly.

"The trans-gender part is fine, I have no problem with trans-gender people at all, I'm not prejudiced. The problem isn't that he is a woman trapped in a man's body." He sighed again. "The problem is that he believes he is a *black* woman trapped in a *white* man's body."

Everyone looked at each other in disbelief. Three people said at once. "Pardon?"

Max took a deep breath. "Here lies the problem. He, or should I say she, is waiting for gender re-assignment surgery and is living as a woman for the next year, you know, to prepare for life as a woman. But, Carl or Carly, wishes to live as a black woman. He/she turned up for the interview in full black-up make-up. In all honesty I thought it was a candid camera spoof at first, but no, she was deadly serious. I thought it inappropriate and frankly racist to have a white person coming into work every day in full black-up make-up. So I politely retracted the job offer. This morning I received a solicitor's letter basically threatening to sue the company for discrimination. So I haven't got a clue what to do. Do I risk offending my black colleagues by allowing a white person to swan around like a black and white minstrel, or do I discriminate against a black woman trapped in a bald middle-age white man's body?"

Everyone in the room looked at each other quite clueless. This was certainly unexpected!

Max's audience sat in a stunned silence. I broke the silence, quietly sliding my hand up. "Are you sure it wasn't a joke?"

He shook his head. "Absolutely no joke. What do you all think? Any idea how I can proceed?" He looked desperately around the room at his stunned audience.

"Well I wear make-up to work all the time and no-one complains." Lola preened.

Stephanie rolled one eye up and one eye down with disapproval. "This is a little different don't you think *Lola*!"

Lola pulled a face at Stephanie's back.

"Okay, for the sake of the company I won't objection to Carl or Carly wearing black-up make-up, as long as it's a sincere belief and she's not doing it in mockery." Tony said thoughtfully.

"That's helpful Tony, thank you." Max said with visible relief.

"I don't really see the problem either." Stan said nodding with Tony. "Look at those black guys in the film 'White Chicks', they wore white-up make-up and no-one batted an eyelid. I can't guarantee I won't laugh till I get used to it though."

Stephanie nodded. "To be honest I've never really understood why it's such a no-no to wear black-up make-up."

"Because in general it *is* racist." Tony said.

"But why is it?" She argued.

He looked a little stumped. "Well, after hundreds of years of black oppression why should the white man get to make a mockery of us?" He seemed pleased with his answer and crossed arms matter of factly.

"Okay, I take your point." She conceded. "But, *women* have been oppressed for *thousands* of years, and you don't see us whining and calling drag queens sexist. Whenever they bung on a wig and a false pair of tits you don't hear us saying they're making a mockery of our femininity do you?"

Stephanie was getting louder and louder and Max was looking more uncomfortable by the second. Several times he tried to change the subject, but Stephanie just talked over the top of him. I shrank down into my seat hoping I wouldn't get dragged into some feminist argument. The only time I ever burned my bra was when I left the iron on it too long.

"On the subject of cross dressing..." Tony was saying. "How is it not sexist that you lot can wear trousers and shirts, yet we can't wear dresses without being called transvestites? Answer me that! It's one rule for you women and another rule for men!"

Stephanie was starting to turn purple with rage. "Men *do* wear dresses, they're called bloody KILTS!" She yelled.

This wasn't going quite how Max had expected it. He and I sat bewildered in the middle of the brawl that ranged from sexism, racism, homophobia, the French, to tights. (Whether wearing black tights counted as blacking up your legs.)

"Don't even get me started on your breast fixation!" Stephanie was pointing to Tony. "I see you peek when you think I aren't looking."

"Well with your eyes I can never see if you *are* looking!" He bellowed back. The room suddenly fell silent with shock at such a personal comment. Everyone normally pretended that they hadn't noticed her eye, though it did often become confusing when trying to tell if she was talking to you or the person next to you.

She flushed purple with rage. "How dare you pick on my disability!"

Tony looked ashamed but found himself backed into a corner and was unable to give up the argument. "A wonky eye is not a disability!" He said sulkily.

"Wonky eye? Do you mean my *optical irregularity*? How dare you say it isn't a disability?"

He muttered under his breath, "Are you talking to me or Stan?"

There was a gasp from everyone as we turned to look at Stephanie for her reaction.

She quietly put her glass of orange juice down on the coffee table and sat back folding her hands calmly onto her lap before saying pleasantly, "I have it on good authority *Tony*, that *you* only have one ball."

Stan laughed before he could help himself and tried to disguise it as a coughing fit.

Tony was livid. "And you *Stephanie*, are probably jealous. One ball or not, I have the tackle to please a woman!" He said grabbing his crotch disgustingly.

"So do I!" She yelled. "Mine might be battery operated but it'll be BIGGER THAN YOURS!"

Once again a stunned silence fell over my living room. Max took the opportunity to bring the debate to a close and herded everyone back out of the front door, thanking them for coming, before slamming the door behind them. He slid down the door until he was sat on the floor, where he rested his arms on his knees and his head in his hands.

"Well that went well." I said helpfully.

No comment from the floor, so I stepped over him and went back through to the lounge to start clearing away the cups and glasses before remembering to top up the fish bowl with some fresh water. Michael (Fish) seemed happy with a water change anyway. I crumbled a little flake food in for him before asking Max if he wanted a cuppa.

"No." Was the reply of the voice from behind the knees.

"By the way," I told the knees, "I got the sack today."

He groaned. "Could this day get any worse?"

"Actually yes, you need to go pick Paul up from his band practice in ten minutes."

Chapter Four

The therapist was looking stressed again. "So let me get this straight. Your husband brought home the woman he was sleeping with and you were more concerned about her seeing your dirty toilet than by her presence in your home?"

I twisted the tissue in my hand into a tight irritated knot. "I don't like people thinking I don't have a clean house."

She gave me a long appraising stare. After what felt like an age she finally spoke. "Weren't you upset?"

"I handled it just fine." I said stiffly.

She didn't look convinced but gestured for me to continue.

***

"The following day I found myself in my usual routine of cooking, ironing and doing Paul's homework that he had forgotten to do the night before. At least I had the rest of the day to myself though now that I was unemployed. While the two pigs troughed through their breakfasts I provided ketchup, then brown sauce, then re-did the toast when it was 'too brown'. (When it came to toast they were definitely racist.)

They drove me mad, I was trying to do history homework and provide waitress services at the same time. Why the hell couldn't they get up and do something for themselves? The twitch in my left eye was re-appearing and I could feel my jaw clenching as the final insult was shouted out by Paul.

"This bacon's too fatty."

Fatty? FATTY? **FATTY???**

I felt a 'pop' in my brain before being flooded with a sense of relief as I filled in the last question on his homework.

Question 12 – What was the name of the head of the German Gestapo during WWII?

I had been about to put Heinrich Himmler, whom I had googled earlier on that morning; instead I wrote – *Herr Flick* – Who used to star in 'Allo 'allo! - Fatty bacon indeed!

***

I pottered about all morning catching up on all the jobs I hadn't previously had time to do. I was just balancing a pile of ironing in one hand while I tried to turn a door handle with the other hand when the phone rang startling me. All hopes of balancing the clothes went out of the window as I dropped them on the floor. "Bugger!" I grumbled before answering the phone.

"Hello?" I asked the receiver.

"Hello!" The robot shouted. **"You have been chosen to receive a government funded boiler…"**

I slammed the receiver down with a bang. Goddam robot rang me up every day.

With a sigh I bent down and started picking up my now crumpled ironing.

By dinnertime I had finished cleaning everything in the house and I was getting bored, so I was quite relieved TLS came home for his dinner unexpectedly. He normally stayed school dinners. I saw his horns pass by the kitchen window before I saw the rest of him come in the back door.

"Hello love." I said.

"Ugh." He said.

"What are you doing home?"

"Ugh, ill."

He did look a little green. "What's the matter?" I said placing a hand over his acne ridden shiny (hairspray covered) forehead, he was burning up.

"Feel sick. Can I go to bed?" He said in a pathetic voice.

"Go on then. I'll ring the school; tell them you won't be in this afternoon." As an afterthought I called after him, "Take a sick bowl up with you!"

"Ugh." He said before returning to the kitchen and rummaging through the pot cupboard.

I got on with making myself a sandwich for my lunch, for once I actually had an appetite.

He walked past me with his sick bowl and headed up the stairs. I was just having the first bite out of my sandwich when I heard him vomit. Thank God I'd made him take a bowl up with him.

I put my sandwich down and went to check on him, see if he needed any tissues or a drink of water. Poor love.

I froze in my tracks as I saw him halfway up the stairs spewing into his sick bowl - that was in reality- my colander! Yellow bile was dripping down through the colander onto my new cream stair carpet.

"Mum?" He said pathetically. "I think I did a boo-boo."

I winked and blinked my irritation at him as I got him into bed and set about cleaning the carpet.

The colander went in the bin along with my un-eaten sandwich.

***

The next thing that happened is a bit of a haze, but I'll try and describe the bits that I do clearly remember before I was dragged off and restrained.

I had just sat down in the lounge to watch '*Escape to the Country*' when there was a knock at the door. I rolled my eyes and groaned and shuffled my slippered feet to the front door where I was met with a double glazing salesman. Brilliant!

"Could I speak to the home owner?" The cheap-suit-clad middle-aged man said.

I rolled my eyes. "That's me, and I don't want double glazing, I *have* double glazing."

"I can see that madam." He barked loudly. "But I see that your front door is *not* double glazed. I can give you a very competitive deal on one of our new units..."

"Let me stop you there." I raised my hand along with my newly acquired temper. "I do *not* want double glazing! I *have* double glazing. If I *wanted* a double glazed door I would have bought one when I bought the windows."

I started to close the door when he put his foot in the way of it stopping me from being able to close it.

"And when did you buy these windows madam? And would you mind telling me how much you paid for them? Are you happy with the quality? We can do you a very competitive deal on windows and doors....We can up-grade your windows to Wilkinson K glass....Finance options are available... How much would you be willing to pay for a new front door?"

As the fuse in my head popped, I took a deep breath...and roared.

"FINE! YOU LIKE TO ASK QUESTIONS ABOUT WHAT I SPEND MY MONEY ON DO YOU? WELL THAT WORKS BOTH WAYS!" I stepped closer to him. He took a step back fearfully. I took a step closer pointing at him. "How much did you pay for that suit?" He took another step back, I took another step forward. "My mother's a tailor, I could get you a good deal on a better suit."

"That's okay Madam." He said with a worried smile. "I'll be going now."

"Oh no you won't!" I grabbed his briefcase. (I don't remember why.)

"Please let go!"

"No!" I grappled for the briefcase handle before kicking him in the shin to make him let go.

His leg went out from under him and he went down like a sack of spuds. I took advantage of my superior position and continued to quiz him. "Why did you buy a black suit but wear brown shoes? Why didn't you get the shoes to match? I can provide you with a pair of black ones for a reasonable fee!" I yelled, stepping back inside and picking up Paul's school shoes from next to the front door, before throwing one of them at the bewildered salesman who was laid across my garden path. "If you can't afford them, I'll do you a finance option!" I bellowed throwing the last one at his head.

I can't really remember much after that, just a bit of a haze while two of my neighbours restrained me and rang for Max. Although they did inform me that I had been ranting and raving to the poor salesman that I could also provide him with a jam-tart that came with a free pube at no extra cost.

Chapter Five

"Hang on a minute." The therapist said looking puzzled whilst shuffling through my notes. "There must be some kind of mix-up; that isn't recorded as the reason for your admittance." She started pulling another folder out of her immense holdall and tutting to herself.

"There's no mistake," I reassured her, "that wasn't the incident that led to the sectioning."

She halted mid-ransacking. "So there's more?"

"Oh yes."

I saw her sneakily looking up to the heavens for help when she thought I wasn't looking. I gritted my teeth and continued....

***

"Max wasn't happy. He didn't have time for my... how did he put it? '*Drama-queen-antics*.'

"It wasn't my fault." I had sulked. "He just wouldn't leave me alone."

"Salesmen are like that!" He said with annoyance. "I know, I am one!"

I muttered that I was sorry and I wouldn't do it again, after which Max decided I should go to bed and sleep off my bad mood while he went back to work.

I tried to go to sleep but my brain had gone into a sudden panic. All day I had the feeling that I had forgotten something, something very important, and I had just remembered what it was. Jean. Jean the homeless lady. Now I no longer worked at the bakers she wouldn't get her bag of leftovers that I usually organised. I sat up in bed in horror. How could I sleep when that old lady was probably starving in her shop doorway? Oh God what sort of person was I to forget her like that! No, I'd have to get up and go take her some food, and then I'd go back to bed and get some sleep. I threw the duvet off me with a huff and got dressed. I could hear soldiers being murdered from Paul's room so he was obviously well enough to play on his x-box.

I slid on my shoes quietly glancing back up the stairs to make sure I wouldn't get caught sneaking out of the house. Paul would be bound to tell on me if Max asked and I'd had enough of being in trouble for one day.

I pulled the door shut carefully behind me and cringed as it shut with a 'click'. Oh no! My heart sank as I realised I'd let the Yale latch drop! God! Now I'd have to knock to get back in. Bugger! Never mind I'd cross that bridge when I got to it, for now the only priority was that poor starving old lady. I bobbed down as I shuffled along the garden path hoping to hide from view of my neighbours behind the small hedge that separated our gardens. I couldn't face them yet I was still too embarrassed. Once I got through the gate I stood up properly, looked about me, discretely pulled my knickers from up my bum where they had become firmly lodged and trotted down the road to catch a bus.

It was too late to go to a bakery and buy the usual things that I gave her; most of the shops were now closed. The only place still open was 'The Big B' our local hamburger takeaway. I stopped in there and filled a bag with an assortment of burgers and chips, plus a salad (I had no idea if she got regular fruit and veg) and of course a big cup of hot tea.

Once I paid for everything I walked the mile or so further into town to the doorway where she normally spent the night. It was just starting to spit with rain as I spotted her huddled in the doorway in the distance. She stood up mistrustfully as I approached her, clutching her dirty holdall against her chest.

"Hi Jean, it's only me; Claire from the bakers."

She didn't say anything, just glared at me from under a layer of grime.

"I've brought you something." I said offering her the bag.

"What is it?" she said eyeing the bag in my outstretched hand warily.

"Just a meal, burgers and chips, bit of salad and a cup of tea."

She nodded her head at me but didn't take the

bag, so I nervously put it on the step and slid it towards her. She bent down slowly reaching for it but never taking her eyes off mine as she felt for the bag. Her wariness of me was obvious so I backed away, nodding my goodbye.

As I was turning away she spoke. "It was you wasn't it?"

"What was?" I asked turning back.

"That paid for my dinners all that time."

I nodded. "I was glad to help; we only need a bit of help at times don't we."

She nodded to me and turned away holding her bag of food trying to look nonchalant about it but I wasn't fooled I could see the eagerness in her shaking hand and the hunger in her eyes.

"Can I take you somewhere? There's a shelter on Rosen Street, I could take you..."

"No!" She interrupted me sharply. "Not going there."

"Why not? You'd be warm and dry."

She put her head down sulkily. "They won't let me take my cat."

I looked down and saw the ginger tabby peering from behind her ripped knee socks.

"Do you like cats?" She asked suspiciously.

I didn't. But I told her that I did. "The trouble is I'm allergic to them."

"Oh." she nodded. There was an awkward silence for a moment before she said, "I'm having my dinner now then."

I took it I was dismissed and bade her goodbye until the day after when I'd bring something else. I turned back to wave, but her back was turned as she tucked into the burger.

I felt much better after that. That awful nagging feeling I'd had all day had finally gone, and I felt much like myself again. I hopped onto the bus feeling like a huge burden had been lifted, however that thought was short lived as I got off the bus and approached my house. I had forgotten that I had locked myself out of the house earlier. That awful sinking feeling came back into my stomach again. I looked at the house next-door cautiously trying to see if anyone had spotted me. They were very nosey people who didn't even seem embarrassed about how nosey they were. If I ever caught them peeping through the fence at me, they just waved and carried on peeping. The coast looked clear but I wasn't taking any chances, so I dropped down behind the hedge again and crawled on my hands and knees down the path towards the back door that I was praying might still be unlocked.

It wasn't.

Bugger! I gave a heavy sigh; I *really* didn't want to ring the bell and have to explain to Max why I'd wandered off when Paul grassed me up. (Which he would.)

I stood back and looked at the house, the top window in the dining room was open, maybe if I could climb up there I could fit through it, drop down the other side and no one would be the wiser to my brief escape. I huffed to myself. Oh well, why not. I just needed something to stand on. I looked about me; all I could see that I could drag over there was the dustbin, which would have to do. I went to pick it up so that I could move it quietly but found it to still be full. "Damn the bin men and their bloody strikes!" I mumbled under my breath. I put the lid back on in frustration and stamped my foot. I looked about me to try and spot something else to use but there was absolutely nothing. Shit! There was nothing else for it. I started emptying the contents out of the bin, one soggy bin bag after another until it was light enough to lift without dragging. I wiped the stinking stale bean juice off my hands down my jeans in disgust, ugh! I carefully lifted it up and tottered with it until it was underneath my dining room window, all the time worrying at how dirty my net curtains looked in this light.

Once I was happy with the position of it I clambered up carefully onto it and pulled the window open as wide as it would go before I hooked my left leg over the sill while grabbing the window frame with my hands for support. Now climbing through a small window is no easy feat, especially not when your feet get tied up in the aforementioned net curtains. I managed to get both legs through but got stuck by the buttocks. I then got into a wee bit of a panic at being stuck by the buttocks half in half out of a small window and started thrashing about a bit. Quite a bit actually. Fortunately, the thrashing about loosened my arse and I dropped down through the opening with a bang into my dining room. God the relief to be free!

I stood up wiping my hands on my jeans and looked up in horror as I was met by the sight of my audience sitting around the dining table watching me. There was TLS (who had gotten out of bed now he was feeling better), Max, (who had come home early to check on me) my two nosey neighbours from next door (who had earlier restrained me,) and my mother. This little group had been sitting at my dining table apparently discussing my strange behaviour earlier when they saw a pair-of-legs appear through the window.

I looked from one stern frowning face to another. No one said a word. My mother deliberately looked at her manicured fingernails as though they had suddenly become fascinating. Max was glaring at me and ever so slightly shaking his head. Paul however looked quite amused and wasn't hiding the fact very well the way his shoulders were shaking and his face had gone puce. Finally, I looked to the two nosey pensioners from next door – Mr and Mrs Little, who looked at me with glee, as though they were willing me to do something to amuse them further. I wouldn't put it past them if they had brought popcorn with them.

I could stand the awkwardness no longer, so I

said, "Would anyone like a cuppa? I'm making one anyway?"

Silence from the audience.

I gathered my dignity, stuck my nose in the air and went to cry in the kitchen.

Once I was out of sight I mopped my wet face with a piece of kitchen roll before blowing my nose and disposing of the tissue into the pedal bin. I turned around rubbing my eyes as I heard Max getting rid of the neighbours through the front door.

"Well thank you for your concern." I heard him say as I peered around the kitchen door and saw Max ushering them out –much to their disappointment the way they were trying to see back around the door that he was closing.

"You will let us know if we can do anything won't you?" They said as he door closed on them.

I shot back across the kitchen before Max could see me peeping. He came in quietly giving me an assessing look. "Do you want to explain yourself?"

I shrugged trying to look nonchalant. "I locked myself out. The window was open…it seemed the logical thing to do."

"The front door was unlocked, I left it unlocked for you when I got home and realised you'd gone out."

"Oh. I didn't know."

He wouldn't let it go. "If you thought the door was locked why didn't you knock?"

Bugger this was getting more like a police interrogation by the minute. "Does it matter?"

"Where did you go?"

"For a walk."

"It's raining."

"It wasn't when I set off!" I was getting angry now. I hate being quizzed. I couldn't tell him the truth of where I'd really been as Max wouldn't approve of my new charity work feeding a homeless woman.

I turned away and turned the taps on filling the washing up bowl hoping that Max would take it that I was done talking.

No such luck. He sent in the big guns instead...my mother.

"Claire!" She bellowed making me jump and drop the cup I'd just been washing up. "What's the meaning of all this nonsense? Shouting at people, assaulting salesmen, and now breaking into houses!"

"*My* house, breaking into *my* house, I'm not a burglar."

"Not yet, but the way you're going it won't be long. I didn't bring you up to be such a...a...Deviant." She tossed her shampoo-and-set back with annoyance.

"I am not a deviant!" I argued turning around to face her. "I've just had a lot on my plate lately."

"And you've been sacked I hear."

I bit my lip and turned back to washing-up. I would not make a scene and argue with my mother, the more you argue with her, the more she argues back. The faster she believes she has won the faster she will leave. I took a deep breath, gritted my teeth and said, "You're right Mum I have been acting a little off, I've had a lot to deal with lately but I'll be fine now I promise."

She raised one neatly groomed eyebrow at me in response.

I carried on. "I mean it, I'll behave now."

She scowled. "Make sure you do! Anymore of this nonsense and you're off to see a therapist. I've given Max the number of a good one. I'll pay. You can pay me back as soon as you get another job." With that she turned on her heels and left through the front door, briefly saying goodbye to Max on the way out.

As soon as she wasn't looking I stuck two fingers up at her and stuck my tongue out.

I heard a laugh from across the room as Paul stood watching me with a new amusement I hadn't seen before. He shook his head. "If you want I'll take you to my hairdressers and get you some horns, that don't half wind mother's up."

I nodded as though I was considering it before smiling and patting him on the shoulder.

Chapter Six

Breakfast the next morning was a little different to normal. I awoke half an hour late to find that someone had turned my alarm clock off. I dragged my clothes on in a panic trying to find a clean pair of jeans through the ironing pile that I hadn't got around to putting away the day before when I had been interrupted by the salesman.

I legged it downstairs expecting to be greeted by chaos, but no. I looked about me in disbelief at the clean and tidy kitchen that contained the two men in my life who were laying out breakfast for me! FOR ME! I was delighted and stood there stunned. Paul was laying out my knife and fork while Max was dishing out pancakes onto a plate for me. Noticing me Paul pulled out a chair and beckoned me to sit down. I smiled and obliged. Max put my plate down in front of me with a nice smile before returning to the oven where he pulled out two plates of bacon and eggs he had been keeping warm in there.

I sat bewildered with a smile on my face as they both sat down. "What's all this in aid of?"

Max looked to Paul before answering, "Well

we've been thinking, you have been under a bit of pressure lately, it can't be nice being sacked like you were, and we just thought we'd make a bit of an effort to cheer you up a bit…just so that you know…we appreciate you."

My heart nearly exploded it suddenly felt so full. I had been sorely in need of a little reassurance lately, just to know that I mattered, even if only a little. I beamed at the pair of them before smiling down into my first bite of strawberry pancake – my favourite.

We all enjoyed a nice family breakfast to-gether laughing at Paul's descriptions of his vari-ous capers at school, and Max was positively charming telling Paul and I about his own school days, some of which I remembered as we went to school together, though some of the stories were new to me too so I laughed along with Paul. It was just like old times again when Paul was little and we used to make him giggle in his high chair. With-out a doubt their efforts had cheered me up no end.

After Paul set off for school I noticed Max's smile slip a little; leaving him looking more wistful than cheerful.

"Penny for them?" I offered.

He looked up a little startled from his daydream. "Oh, it's just that Carly starts work today, and I've got no idea how things are going to go at work."

I was curious. "What's Carly like? You know apart from the blacking-up?"

"Really nice. Polite, sweet, rather feminine to say she's going through the change quite late by usual standards. I wouldn't be worried; she'd fit right in with everyone if it wasn't for this insistence that she is really a black woman in a white body. I've been to lots of anti-discrimination seminars over the years and courses on how to prevent discrimination in the workplace but I've never come across a situation like Carly's before." He sighed and rubbed his eyes. "What if someone makes a complaint about her blacking-up? Do I get sued for allowing her to black-up? What if she sues me – like she already said she could, for discriminating against her rights? It's a mine field and I think I'm gonna put my foot in it no matter where I step." He looked down despondently.

I got up and patted him on the shoulder. He looked surprised though pleased, but then again I suppose I'm not a very touchy feely sort of person lately.

I said, "I'm sure you'll muddle through it, we're all just people trying to carve a life out for ourselves; just be sensitive and speak honestly and you'll be fine. All anyone ever wants is to be treated with respect; it doesn't matter whether you wear a thong or a jockstrap."

He smiled and kissed me on the cheek as he left - the first real intimacy there had been between us for more than a year. I flushed and put my hand to the kiss's imprint as he left.

***

Once I was alone I found myself at somewhat of a loose end; there's only so many times you can scrub a house top to bottom before you have to admit that it is finally clean. I made myself a cup of coffee and picked up the newspaper off the doormat taking it through to the kitchen with me. I opened it to the job section hoping to see a new career option leap out at me and poured over the ridiculously titled jobs. *'Waste management and Disposal Technician.'* Since when was a bin man a technician? I shook my head and carried on. *'Modality Manager'.* I had to google that one, it meant nurse!

'Media distribution officer.' It took me a little while to work that one out. (Paperboy.) *'Transparency enhancement facilitator.'* Window cleaner! It was ridiculous.

After I'd got sick to death of googling the various job titles to try and identify what they really were, I decided I'd just go down to the job centre tomorrow instead where they could translate the ridiculous titles into normal job descriptions.

I flicked past the job vacancies and onto the classifieds. I browsed over various pieces of antique furniture that I would love to buy if I had a house big enough for a chaise longue and a matching love seat. I wrinkled my nose up as my fantasy of lying out on a velvet chaise longue whilst eating a Cadbury's Flake turned into a nightmare of TLS dry-humping his girlfriend on it while I'm out. "Ugh!" I gave an involuntary shudder. I didn't approve of 'The Girlfriend'. I know she had a name, (Jenny) but I couldn't think of her as anything other than 'The Girlfriend' with air quotes. I know they say all mother's disapprove of their son's girlfriends but this one was a real piece of work. School skirt far higher than regulations allowed, blouse unbuttoned to show off her huge bosom. She positively hypnotised him with them, or rather tit-notised him as I privately thought; leaning over him all of the time when they are supposed to be doing homework. With the amount of chemistry that's going on between them I just hope it doesn't graduate to biology. And she's older; almost a year older. Plus, I think she knows I don't like her because she's always really nice to me, too nice. I can't tell if she's being sarcastic or not. For example, the other day she looked down at my pink trainers and said "Cool." Complimentary? Sarcastic? I'm not sure. She then went on to say, (after learning about a high speed sprint I performed to catch a bus) "You're so lucky having such a small chest; I could never run for a bus with mine." Ouch!

All thought of Jenny's knockers went out of the window as the phone started ringing, disturbing me from my daydreaming.

"Hello?" I answered.

A polite Indian sounding accent replied, "Hello, is this Claire Porter?"

"Yes." I said inwardly groaning. Everyday lately I get called and told that my credit card has been cancelled and I have to give them all of my bank details over the phone so that my card can be reinstated. Do they really think I'm that stupid?

"Hi Claire, my name is Bob, how are you today?"

I was irritated; he could barely pronounce Bob; it didn't roll off his tongue as one's own name should. Why do foreign cold callers always give themselves English names? But, what I hate even more is when someone you don't know asks how you are. That winds me up something wicked. I'd normally force a polite tone into my voice, swallow my irritation and be nice until they went away.

Not today though.

I could feel irritation rising up through my PMT-ridden belly. Today was going to be different.

"Bob you say." I said. "What's that short for?"

Silence at the other end of the line.

"Hello? Bob? Are you there?"

"Erm, yes Madam, sorry there was a problem with the line there for a second. I was just calling to…"

"Hold on." I interrupted him. "I asked a question. What is Bob short for?" I bit my lip as I waited patiently for him to finish panicking.

"Pardon?"

"I said, *what* is Bob short for?"

After a few seconds he replied, "Bobert."

I covered the receiver while I snorted down it.

Once composed I said, "Thanks, Bobert."

Obviously pleased to get back on track Bobert continued with his script. "How are you today Madam?"

I was ready for this one.

"Well *Bobert*, I have had the most awful period pain I've ever had in my life! And don't get me started on the flow rate I'm experiencing! Between you and me, the consistency isn't very pretty either."

Silence from the other end of the phone. I grinned. Serves him right for asking a personal question, next time he might be prepared for a personal answer. That might make him think twice before asking people personal questions in the future!

I was surprised when he came back on the line.

"I'm sorry to hear of your troubles Madam, but I am calling from Griffin High School, I have your son here with me in the medical unit, he's been sick and wishes to come home. Would you be able to come and collect him?"

I felt the colour drain from my face. I had believed I was speaking to someone from Bombay or somewhere that wished to rob me of my credit card details, not my son's school nurse who I would now have to go face!

I stammered down the phone. "Sorry Bobert, I'm on my way!"

It seems Max wasn't the only inadvertent racist in the family.

Chapter Seven

After putting the phone down on Bobert I rang for a taxi to take me to the school. Whilst I was waiting for it to arrive I slid on a pair of dark glasses and pulled on an old woollen hat over my hair. It was still pretty cold for April so I didn't look completely stupid. I just felt the need for a bit of camouflage after the previous phone call with the nurse.

I gave myself one last 'how could you be such an idiot' look in the mirror as I hurried outside and got into the waiting taxi.

"Where to then love?" My fat balding chauffer asked as I got myself settled into the back seat, slightly balking at the overpowering air-freshener.

"Griffin High school please."

"Aren't you a little old love?"

It was a good job I was wearing dark glasses so that he didn't see me roll my eyes.

"Got kids there then eh?" He continued.

"A son."

"Better a son than a daughter. I've got two of 'em."

How do you respond to that? I didn't have to, he carried on.

"Thirteen and fourteen they are, and what a pair of madams I can tell you."

He prattled on for the rest of the journey with various anecdotes about his girls. How they fought, cried, whinged and how manipulative they could be when trying to get their own way. I almost butted in with, 'At least they don't put pubes in your jam tarts.' But managed to bite my tongue before it popped out.

I was ever so relieved to get out of the cab at the other end until I remembered I would now have to face Bobert. My stomach heaved as I swung the main school door open and that awful school smell hit me. What is it about that smell that can make you feel about twelve again? I took shallow breaths as I found my way down the corridor towards the nurses' station, noting the three small students waiting outside of the headmaster's office with glum faces. Poor mites I remember that feeling well. I almost said to them as I passed 'Never mind, one day you'll grow up and leave this place forever.' But how could I say that? One day one of them might be here, having to apologise to a school nurse for mistaking them for a cold caller and telling them all about their menstrual cycle.

I took a deep breath and knocked on the door marked 'Medical Unit'.

"Come in." Said the voice through the chipboard door.

I slinked in through the door with my head down

in shame. The young Asian nurse was sitting at his desk eating a wagon wheel as I came in.

"Mrs Porter?" He said through a mouth full of marshmallow.

"Yes, hello." I half smiled/half grimaced as I sat down on the seat that I was offered. He looked a little wary of me but was obviously used to dealing with strange parents so seemed to take me in his stride. He put his wagon wheel wrapper in the bin before speaking.

"Paul was feeling sickly earlier and so I brought him down here to have a lay down until he felt better, but he's been sick several times now so I feel he would be better going home and having a few days off."

"That's fine. I have a taxi waiting outside to take him home. He was sick yesterday too, but he seemed fine when he got up this morning. I thought it must have been a twenty-four-hour bug or something."

He nodded. "There is a stomach-bug going about at the minute, several students have come down with it." He stood up and walked across the room to a door I hadn't noticed earlier. "Paul." He called through the doorway. "Your mum's here, you can go home now."

A pale green Paul staggered dramatically through the doorway like Quasimodo dragging his hump. I have been sick many, many times in my life and not once has it made me walk like the Elephant man.

"What's wrong with your legs?" I asked.

"Ugh. Ill!" was the reply.

Bobert and I shared a glance that involved raised eyebrows and a shake of the head.

"Come on you, let's get you home." I said patting him on the back as he dragged his legs past me like a dog with a sympathy limp.

"Thanks Bob." I said on my way out. But to my immense embarrassment he wasn't done with me.

"No problem Mrs Porter," He dropped his voice. "And I am truly sorry to hear of your menstruating problems. If it's bothering you that much perhaps you should contact your local GP."

I cringed and agreed before leaving, dragging a mortified Quasimodo into the waiting taxi.

***

I got Quasi settled into his bedroom (pit) ensuring that this time he had a suitable receptacle to vomit into. I pulled his quilt up to his bum fluff that he proudly called his goatee and left him to go back to sleep in peace. There was just one problem with Paul being off school ill, I still had to go back out to take food to Jean. I had my eye on the clock trying to work out how much time I had before Max got home. I winced, I would be cutting it fine, it had thrown my day out having to drop everything and go to the school to get Paul. If I set off now though, I should just get back in time before Max got back. But what to do about Paul?

After much deliberation, I wrote a note saying 'Gone to shops won't be long.' And stuck it on the fridge under my alphabet magnets which currently spelt out 'Tits'. I groaned and reshuffled them into something less vulgar. 'Tots' there that was better.

I was just hunting out my shoes when the doorbell rang.

"Oh God now what?" I grumbled and stumbled opening the front door impatiently.

Two black-suit-clad Jehovah's Witnesses! Oh just lovely! This was the third set of religious nutters this week, (although at least the Hare-Krishna were colourful). They beamed at me as only the devoutly brainwashed can. Holding their pamphlets to their double breasted suits as though they were shields against the insults they must get bombarded with.

"Yes what?" I snapped.

"Hello Miss, have you heard the good news?" The first one said proffering his pamphlet at me.

I pursed my lips with annoyance. "I'm not interested, sorry."

I went to close the door but the second one put his foot in the way. I glared down at the intruding foot as its owner carried on where the first one had stopped.

"You're not interested in hearing how God loves you and is preparing to save us all?"

"There's no such thing as God." I argued kicking at his foot that was blocking my door frame.

He laughed. "Of course there is a God. Many people in this day and age have doubts about God due to the wars, famine, etc. But he is coming to save us all. If I could you just refer you to chapter twenty-one, verses three to four of the bible..."

My patience was snapping thread by thread, I had one hour to get to Jean and get back home before Max got back, so I had to close this crap down quickly. I'd been thinking long and hard about religion recently and so I was quite confident as I engaged them in battle.

"Okay fine," I said feeling the adrenalin kicking in as I pulled myself up to my full five foot two height, "assuming that you *are* right and there is a God, why would you want to worship him?"

"I beg your pardon Madam?"

"Well let me put it this way, God is the all-seeing almighty is he not?"

"He is." They agreed nodding to each other.

"And he is capable of anything; he did after all create the earth in six days did he not?"

"He did."

"So, he could intervene and save any number of people from any number of bad situations couldn't he?"

"God works in mysterious ways." The first one shook his head at me as though I was a dim wit. "God has his own wonderful plans for us. It's not for us to know the mind of God."

I rubbed my eyes with frustration. "You see that's where I have a problem with it. For example, I have a goldfish in there." I beckoned back into my house. "I rescued that fish from a cat in the garden that was about to eat it. I saved him, nurtured him, gave him a comfortable home to live in, I change his water regularly and give him good food. When he gets too big for his fish bowl I'll buy him a bigger tank. He's never grovelled at my feet for saving him, and I would never expect him to. Yet as far as that fish knows I am God, and I do a damn sight better job of being God to him than your God does to you." I was getting mad and into my stride by the time they started to try to (unsuccessfully) butt in. I continued. "If I had the powers that *your* God does I would save EVERYONE. I would intervene with guidance, kindness, tolerance and human decency. Therefore, I believe if there is a God he should bow down and worship me for I think I'd make a better one than him!" I was getting loud again and they were looking more and more uncomfortable by the minute.

"Let me ask you," I shouted over the top of suit number two who tried to interrupt me. Grabbing him by his lapels I demanded, "Take 9-11 for instance; if you… what's your name?"

"Peter." He replied meekly trying to detach me from his suit.

"Right Peter, if you had God's power and knowledge for one day on the eleventh of September 2001, would you have intervened?"

"It was God's plan." He replied stubbornly.

"NO IT WASN'T." I countered. "Apparently that was ALLAH's plan!"

No reply. But I wasn't letting them off that easy. "I'll ask you both this time; would you have intervened and saved all of those people if you could?"

Suit number one said yes, at the same time suit number two said no. They looked at each other in panic.

"You," I said to suit number one. "You would save the thousands of people from dying. Well done you, you are a kind and decent human being. And you," I tightened my grip on suit number two, "You would let thousands of people die despite being able to prevent it?"

He looked away without answering.

"How would you know that God wasn't testing you? What if God wanted you to save thousands of people yet you had knowingly allowed them to die?"

He looked in panic to suit number one who shrugged at him, obviously meaning 'dig your way out of that one; you're on your own'.

I let go of suit number two and carried on determined to end the conversation as quick as possible. "If I had the power to save thousands of people I would do so without a second thought, that makes me better than your God. A God that allows bad things to happen to good people can worship my arse!"

I then kicked suit number two's foot from out of the door and slammed it.

***

I sighed shaking my head as I sought out my handbag and coat from the cupboard. What was wrong with me lately? Why couldn't I reign in my thoughts anymore?

I had been bothered by the God-squad many times before and not lost my temper like that.

I think they had just hit a raw nerve, as I said, I have been thinking a lot about the possibility of God lately and just getting more and more angry at the things people do in the name of religion.

Religion to me is simply following a moral compass, being kind to people and treating people how you yourself would want to be treated. Not 'my gang's bigger than your gang' which is all religion seems to be about these days. I don't have a problem with people believing in some all-seeing almighty, I just can't play along with setting a place at the table for other people's invisible friend.

I left it five minutes before I set off as I didn't want to bump into the bible-bashers on my way out. I had a quick peep out of the curtains to check that they had gone and then groaned as I saw they hadn't. They were sat on my garden wall looking at each other with a puzzled, baffled expression on their faces. I grimaced, but had no choice but to go around them. I pulled the door closed quietly behind me and tiptoed down my garden path hoping not to disturb them. I made awkward eye contact with them as I closed the gate behind me. They both looked like their sat-nav had suddenly broken down in the middle of a foreign country. I felt awful.

I looked at my watch, raised my eyebrows at them and said, "Sorry, I have a bus to catch, but, good luck with everything." I then gave them the thumbs up and legged it up the road.

Chapter Eight

Things were going much better by the following week. I had set up a standing order with my former employer so that Jean would still get her daily rations from the bakers; my mother was on holiday and had lost her mobile phone at the airport and so was completely unable to bug me for the next week; and.... Max trapped his Willy in the zipper of his onesie and could barely pee, let alone titillate his tart! So, perhaps there is a God after all!

For the first time in ages I was starting to feel more like my old self again. Not confident and brave or anything dramatic like that, but I was walking a little taller and smiling a little wider. Life was getting a little brighter again.

I sprawled out on the sofa in the living room with a bag of monster munch (that I had stolen from Paul's stash), and was getting ready to watch my new favourite programme *Escape to the Country.* I was quite starting to enjoy this unemployed lark if I'm being honest. I had been on several promising job interviews which had sadly fallen flat after they had spoken to my previous employer for a reference. I take it my reference must have gone something like:- *Very punctual, conscientious worker who garnishes the pastries with pubic hair, whilst wearing inadequate novelty footwear.* I was certainly never asked to attend a second interview anyway.

So after being in full time employment for the past twenty years my life was suddenly my own. The first few days I was climbing the walls with boredom, but I soon settled into a routine of *Homes under the Hammer, This Morning, Loose Women, Flog It,* and then *Countdown.*

I was still applying for jobs, but thoroughly enjoying having time to myself. On day three I spent four hours in the bath! I just kept heating it up every time it went cold. By the time I got out I looked like I'll probably look when I'm eighty, pink and wrinkly. Plus, for once Max had to get a cold shower as I had stolen all of the hot water!

Once I had finished picking all of the bits of monster munch out of my belly button I realised that I could hear a strange noise outside. I turned the TV down while I cocked my head to one side and listened, mm I was sure I heard something. I wiped the crumbs away and got up to peek out of the window and then crapped myself with fright at the wrinkled face that was staring back at me through the net curtain. Mr Little from next door had his face jammed up against my front room window. "Good God!" I proclaimed. "You scared me half to death!" I mimed a heart attack through the glass.

"Just wondered if you were in." He mimed back; his wig wobbling precariously.

"Why didn't you just knock on the door?" I gestured.

"I didn't want to disturb you if you were busy."

I shook my head and finally found the window catch to open it. "Did you want me for something?"

"No." He said. "Just wondered if you were in that's all."

With that, he toddled off back up my garden path. I shook my head incredulously after him. I know I can be a little odd at times but my neighbours are definitely weirder than me. However, while I was looking out of the window I did see a BT Open reach van parked outside my house blocking off our driveway. It must be for someone else I thought, as there was nothing wrong with my phone lines. I picked my phone up to check, and yes, there was the dial tone as normal. I just hoped the van would be gone before Max came home; he went mental about people parking over our driveway entrance.

Satisfied, I put the phone back in its cradle and went back to see if the couple from Hertfordshire were going to go for the mystery house or the barn conversion.

It was around an hour later when I was in the middle of Paul's history homework -googling the chronological order of Henry VIII's wives, when suddenly my internet connection dropped.

"What the hell?" I asked the lap top. I started tapping buttons trying to get the internet to pop back up but to no avail. After checking my phone for a dial tone a few minutes later I realised that my phones were now dead too. It didn't take me long to find out that the BT Open reach maintenance man had accidently cut through my phone lines whilst he had been repairing the phone lines for the house over the road. However, I found this out ten minutes after he had driven off!

I was furious. I hadn't felt the rage in my belly for the past week and thought that I had gotten the last of the aggression out of my system venting at the God squad the previous week. I pulled my mobile phone out of my pocket and rang the operator for the phone number of BT. After carefully writing down the number I had been given by the operator I hung up and typed in the number for BT. A robot asked me to type in the phone number that I was calling from before demanding me to type in my account number. "I don't have one." I told it.

It replied with, "Please say or enter your account number now."

"I don't have one."

"Did you say...you are getting one? Was that correct?"

I was getting seriously annoyed with R2 bleeding D2. "No. That's not correct I don't have an account number."

"Did you say...yes?"

"NO!" I bellowed down the phone with annoyance.

"Please say which service you wish to speak about, for example...BROADBAND, PHONE, TELEVISION."

"Phone."

"Connecting you to...BROADBAND."

"UGH!!!" I fumed.

After ten minutes of listening to deafening music while I was on hold I finally got through to an operator.

"Hello cwoud ayou peses tel pe accont nemer peas?" A thick foreign accent asked me. It took a few seconds for my brain to translate the garbled statement into – "Hello could you please tell me your account number."

"I don't have one." I told him. "I'm not a BT customer, my account is with SKY, but your BT engineer just came out to fix my neighbour's phone and cut me off at the same time!"

He replied with something that I believe was – "I am very sorry to hear that but as you are not a BT customer there is nothing I can do. I suggest you call your own service provider to complain."

"But *they* didn't cut me off, YOU DID!"

I've no idea what he said next as I couldn't understand a word of it.

"I'm sorry," I said, "I can't understand your accent could I please speak to an English operator?"

"I am terminating this call as you are using offensive racist language." He then cut me off.

I stared at my phone, gobsmacked with shock at being called a racist. "How is it racist to say that you can't understand someone's accent?" I was bewildered.

Next I tried calling SKY. After several more conversations with robots I finally got through to an operator –who had such a thick Scottish accent that I couldn't understand him either. He also found my Yorkshire accent difficult to understand, so it took around an hour to get my point across. After many 'Pardon?s' on both sides I was told that no-one could come out and fix my phone line for a week! Bloody brilliant! So much for my stress free happy equilibrium, now I was twice as stressed as I was before! My left eye was twitching and winking so fast that I felt like it was dictating some sort of Morse code to the other eye which was blinking its own demented reply in return. I winked and twitched my way over to the sofa to have a lie down and try to calm my kangarooing face. I tried to concentrate on just breathing calmly, deep breaths in and out, in and out. I put my fingers on my throat to feel my pulse and was worried by how fast it was racing and how *loud* it seemed. I could hear it distinctly banging away in my jugular before feeling foolish at the realisation that it was actually my bloody watch I could hear ticking. I tutted at myself in disgust. How had my day gone from being great to shit in the space of an hour? My head was starting to pound like a snare drum with the stress. I would seriously have to get my temper under control before Max got home. He'd already told me one more unreasonable outburst and I'd be sent to the shrink. What is it with these sudden rage attacks? What the hell is wrong with me?

Chapter Nine

I could see the therapist was looking bored at me and trying to stifle a yawn. I took a break from talking for a while and took a sip from the glass of water at the side of me. (Plastic glass I noted.) After what seemed like an age finally she spoke.

"You seem to have a worry of being portrayed as a racist. Where does this fear comes from do you think?"

She caught me off guard with that one. "I don't know. Racism and sexism is all the media seems to talk about these days. Half of the things that are deemed racist I would never have thought of as being racist. I suppose it makes me worry that maybe I'm a racist and just don't know it."

The therapist looked at me closely leaning forward. "Tell me the first instance you remember of thinking you might be a racist."

I thought about it for a moment. "Well, I don't think there's anything in particular. To be honest I think maybe it's because I grew up with a racist bigot of a mother and I've always been terrified of turning out like that."

"In what way do you think your mother is a

racist?"

"Oh I don't just *think* she's a racist, she *is* a racist." I looked away cringing at the memories that flooded my brain, filling my face with a shamed flush. "Okay, here's an example for you." I paused before ploughing on. "When I was about nine we were out shopping when we bumped into an old friend of hers from school who was shopping with her own daughter –who was mixed race. The friend introduced her daughter to us and we all had a nice chat before going our separate ways. As we walked away my mum said 'what a pretty little girl, such a shame she's one of *those*, but then again the poor little mite can't help it can she.' I was speechless, even at that age I knew that was a terrible thing to say."

The therapist looked taken aback.

"See what I mean." I said. "When I was little we lived next to a family who had dwarfism. They were just a nice normal family who happened to be small." I took a deep breath. "My mother used to refer to them as the midget gems, and whistle *'high-ho'* when she saw them coming up the garden path. She referred to their house as Lilliput and convinced my little sister that the small father next door was the tooth fairy." I hid my face beneath my hands with shame.

"The family next door were always baffled when my little sister would turn up at their door holding out her hand for them to view the tooth sitting in the palm of her hand. Though to be fair I think they thought she was 'special'. I once heard them refer to her as 'the little retard from next-door'."

The therapist looked speechless. "From your description of your mother it sounds as though she was a...dominant personality."

"That's putting it mildly. Let me see, what else did she say...Oh yes, here's another one. She once humiliated me at a parents evening by shouting loudly, 'do we have to go see *that* butch lesbian PE teacher?' And she actually pointed out who she meant. My PE teacher wasn't a lesbian, *HE* was man; he just had collar length hair and delicate calves. But more to the point, he heard her, and after that he had it in for me all year."

The therapist flicked through her notes before stopping on the last page. "Okay, well we seem to have gone off topic a bit here, can we set these issues with racism aside a moment and get back the incident in question that led to your...breakdown."

I sighed. "Sure why not."

***

Okay, so after a week had passed we still had no telephone or internet, my mother was back from holiday, and Max was back to getting his twinkie-stinky. So all-in-all I was feeling the pressure a bit. Plus I had a disaster of an interview (interrogation) with the job centre where they demanded to know why every interview I went to turned into a catastrophe.

"You've been for six interviews in the past week." the snotty, pimply little weasel behind the desk had asked me. "Could you explain to me why on your last job interview you were escorted off the premises for using foul language?" He sat back in his chair with a smug self-satisfied smirk. "I hope you don't think that by sabotaging your interviews you can stay on job seekers allowance."

How dare he! I could feel my heart starting to beat a little quicker as I answered, "It went downhill when they wanted to know about the pube in the jam tart."

"I beg your pardon?" Smug face said.

"They asked the reason why I was fired from my last job."

He stared at me blankly. "You put a pube in a jam tart?"

"I did NOT!" Came the roar from my face.

"So you were framed? With a …pube?" he said the last word with a hush looking around him to see if he'd been overheard saying the word 'pube'.

I hung my head in shame. "It's complicated." I looked up to see his harsh stare. "Hey don't look at me like that, I didn't do it and it wasn't even my pube." Okay, I definitely said that too loud, I was getting looks from the waiting queue.

He shook his head still staring at me. "So you mentioned this 'incident' in your interview then?

What was their reaction?"

I was starting to grit my teeth as I answered. "What would you say if you owned a bakery and someone came in for an interview who had been sacked for putting a pube in a jam tart? They wouldn't listen to me when I said I didn't do it. They called me a..." I took a deep breath. "They called me a pervert!"

Smug face laughed out loud. He actually laughed out loud. I get called a pervert and he thinks it's funny? I completely lost it and before I could think straight I lunged for him. I wanted to wipe that smug grin from off his face, so I had grabbed him by the tie and stapled it to his desk.

Suffice to say I was escorted from the building and told that there would be an investigation – though as I was led off I shouted to my audience, "I am not a pervert!"

***

By the time I got to the bus stop I was absolutely fine again. Well, maybe not fine but I at least had myself under control. Maybe I was having some kind of mid-life crisis? Or was it just that my life had spiralled from out of my control? Was this extenuating circumstances? Have I lost the plot? All these things I pondered as I rode the bus home.

I was awoken from my slump by my mobile phone ringing in my pocket.

"Hello?" I asked it.

"Is this Mrs Porter?"

"Yes?" I said wearily, expecting someone to be trying to sell me PPI or something.

"My name is Eric Manners I'm your son's careers advisor."

"Oh, hello. Is everything okay?" What the hell did he want now?

"Everything's fine, I just wondered if I could pop around tomorrow afternoon and discuss a few things with you if that's convenient?"

Oh God! I thought, but "Oh yes that's fine." is what I said.

"Wonderful, I'll see you tomorrow about two o'clock then."

"Okay, see you tomorrow."

I hung up. What the hell was this about then?

***

I decided to get off the bus early and call in to see Max at his workplace. I normally avoided the place like the plague but I think I just needed to see a friendly face. Okay maybe not friendly, but familiar at least. I swung the large glass door open and was assaulted by the stale perfumed air wafting around the building. I grimaced at the pan-piped music that greeted me as I exited the elevator. Stephanie spotted me from her desk across the foyer and waved enthusiastically. At least I believed it was at me, with her 'optical irregularity' it was hard to tell.

"Claire!" She greeted me with delight. "What

brings you here?"

"Oh you know, just popped in to say hello. Is Max around?"

She looked slightly panicky. "Oh he's around here somewhere." She said with a nervous laugh, looking involuntarily at the stationary cupboard across the hall.

"I bet he is." I replied with a grimace.

Stephanie patted my hand gently. "He doesn't deserve you ya know? You're really special Claire." she stroked my hand a little too meaningfully.

Oh, no. She was giving me the eye! (No pun intended.) I extricated my hand as quickly as possible. "So is Max around?"

"He's in a meeting...with Lola." She raised her eyebrows meaningfully.

"Fine." I said through gritted teeth, "I'll wait."

"Look love, we're all grown-ups here. You obviously know what's going on. Dump the bastard. Trust me, a penis is over-rated!"

"I'm sorry I don't know what you're talking about. But I have to go now; I just remembered there's something I have to do."

I was out of there like a shot. I had no intention of discussing my tattered remnants of a marriage with Stephanie or anyone else for that matter. Although she had a point about his penis being over-rated.

On exiting the building, I turned down the path that snaked around the building. Spotting a little bench unoccupied, I sat down and sat with my head resting on my knees.

"Tough day love?" Asked a voice from the shadows of the building in front of me.

I looked up startled, seeing no-one.

"Sorry, I didn't mean to make you jump." The voice said as a strange looking black woman holding a cigarette emerged from the shadows.

It was Carly.

Chapter Ten

"Hi, Claire isn't it?" She asked in a husky brummy accent.

"Yes, and you must be Carly." I said shaking her outstretched hand, feeling briefly jealous of her immaculate manicure.

"I recognised you from the photos on Max's desk." She explained. "How did you know who I was?"

I panicked. I only knew of one transgender who wore black-up make-up.

"I'm just messing with you." She said laughing pleasantly. "I get that I have a '*distinctive look*'."

That was one word for it. Subtlety was obviously not her style. From her *Tina Turner* wig to her red stilettos it was obvious she had confidence and wasn't afraid of standing out. I wished I had an ounce of her confidence.

"I'm sorry; it's just that I've heard a lot about you."

"I bet you have. It's okay, I get it a lot."

"So... how are you settling in?" I racked my brain for something to say whilst trying my hardest not to stare at her amazing shoes.

"It's okay. But if I'm honest I don't really get on that well with your Max."

"Oh, well…neither do I actually." I nodded earnestly. "In fact I think he's a shit-head."

"Me too." She said with delight. She paused and looked me up and down for a moment. "Me and a few of the girls are going out tonight…you know, girls' night. Do you… want to come?"

I stared back at her glamorously painted face and said. "Why not!"

***

The club seemed deafening as we waited outside in the queue. I was a little nervous of what to expect having never been to a gay bar before. In fact, to be honest I hadn't been to a bar of any kind for maybe fifteen years, and I had never been much of a drinker. I had deliberated for an hour over what to wear. Carly was so glamorous, what would she think of my sensible ankle-length full-sleeved frocks? She'd never know, as I cut three foot off the bottom of my turquoise 'Sunday dress' and wore that. I felt a little self-conscious at my lily-white legs and briefly wondered if -now Carly and I were friends, that she would lend me some of her black-up make-up for them? Probably too early to ask I thought, so instead I sprayed copious amounts of fake tan on them. (Which didn't seem to colour them one damn bit.)

So there I stood in the queue, feeling like my arse was hanging out and cringing at how my knees looked. As well as Carly and I, Stephanie had tagged along –although no-longer giving me the glad eye thankfully; a rather glamorous straight drag queen called Terry (Terri?) and another straight woman who worked alongside Stephanie called Emma. Apparently they'd all been coming to this club every-week for the past month.

"Why do you go to a gay bar all of the time if you consider yourself a straight woman?" I had asked Carly earlier.

She looked at me as though I was naïve, (and I was.)

"This place is a lot more open minded than a lot of places. It's easier to be accepted and to just... BE in a place like this. The world *is* changing for the better, *slowly*, but it's still a way to go for some of us."

I could understand that.

Four Pina-colada's later and I was in heaven. I had an absolute blast. Everyone in the place was in a good mood, the music was terrible and the décor was tacky but my god what an atmosphere! I never had so much fun before. I no-longer cared about my lily-white legs which were on full show as I pole danced around a plastic palm tree while the rest of the club cheered. I even had a great time with Stephanie who admitted she'd only been hitting on me to wind me up in the hope that it got back to Max and annoyed him.

As we all left the club for the long walk home we

were crying and snorting with laughter at the song we'd made up.

> *'We know a man named Max,*
> *his hygiene is a little lax.*
> *He likes to stare at ladies' chests,*
> *which makes us want to wear our vests.*
> *We're told he has a little nob,*
> *if we say it - we will lose our job....'*

It was crap in retrospect I know, but our drunken brains thought it was hilarious. Unfortunately, it was a long walk home and one thing led to another. By the time we got to my road we were singing a rendition of *Copa Cabana.*

> *'Her name was Lola,*
> *She was a slow girl.*
> *With chicken feathers in her hair and*
> *dress made out of pubic hair.*
> *She's crap at typing and doing filing*
> *And while she tries to be a whore*
> *She never charges any more....'*

You get the gist.

As we approached my house I whispered "Shh-hhh." (at the top of my lungs.)

Stephanie and Emma ignored me and carried on with our rendition of *Copa Cabana.*

> *'Rashes from 'taches and boiling hot flashes*

At the Copa...they felt her muff...'

As I crept up my stairs to bed I could still hear them off in the distance. Grinning to myself I carefully got undressed and into bed beside the sleeping figure of Max.

"Good night?" He asked making me jump.

"Er yep. I thought you were asleep." I slurred.

"It's hard to sleep when you're being serenaded with a song about your inadequate genitals!" With that he turned over in a huff and ignored me.

Whoops! I thought he would've been asleep and wouldn't hear us. Oh well, never mind. Sod him.

***

The next morning it felt as though my head was being used for a swarm of bees to nest in. What the hell was I thinking drinking that much? I felt sick as a pig and I wanted the ground to open up and swallow me whole. I had pole danced around a palm tree! Me! I was now a pole dancer!

Never again.

I got up to find that Max and TLS had already left so at least it gave me chance to recover in piece. While I was waiting for the kettle to boil I re-arranged the fridge magnets again, changing them from 'Vulva' to 'Volvo'. There, that was better. Underneath it was the word 'Tit'. There was no point altering it, every time I changed it to 'tot', someone changed it back again within minutes.

After vomiting a few times and having an hour long bath I started to feel a little better…that is until I remembered that Paul's careers advisor would be arriving soon.

"Shit, shit, shit!" I cursed. That was just what I needed while I had a colossal hang-over. I quickly dressed as I realised that the clock was racing towards two o'clock.

Low and behold, at five to two, there went my door bell.

I was almost leaning on the front door as I opened it to find the elegantly dressed, attractive man on my doorstep clutching his briefcase and looking baffled.

"There's a pair of knickers in your rose bush." He said.

"Pardon?" I asked.

"There." He said pointing to the left of the front door.

I looked in horror at the shocking pink thong hanging from the rose bush beside my door.

"Are they yours?" He asked with amusement.

"Absolutely not!" I was horrified and not entirely sure if I was being honest. I had been wearing a pink thong last night.

"You'd better come in." I said wearily holding the door open.

"That's very kind of you thank you."

"Would you like a cup of tea, or coffee?" I asked.

"A cup of tea would be wonderful if you're sure

you don't mind?"

"I'm making one anyway." I replied. "Do you want me to hang your coat up?"

He shrugged out of his coat and handed it to me.

"Just pop through to the lounge and make yourself comfortable while I bring the tea."

"I'm not used to such hospitality." He grinned. "Actually, would you mind terribly if a colleague of mine joined us? He's just around the corner. It would be very useful for his input; he really is an excellent teacher."

"That's fine I suppose." I said with a shrug.

"I'll just give him a quick call now." He said, fishing his mobile phone from his pocket and heading through to the lounge. I filled up the kettle and leant my head against the cool fridge door for comfort while I waited for the kettle to boil.

Just as they kettle began to rattle the doorbell went again. "God he *was* around the corner." I mumbled as I pulled the door open.

"Hi." The bespectacled man on the doorstep said. "I'm here about Paul's career choices."

"It's okay," I told him. "I knew you were on your way. Would you like a cup of tea or coffee?"
After ascertaining what he wanted, I sent him through to the living room while I made the tea.

As I entered the room I saw them both looking at our family photos on the mantelpiece.

"He's a fine boy." The first teacher said. I had forgotten to ask his name.

"Oh he is." Said the second one who I took to be Eric (by the laminated name badge) with whom I had spoken with yesterday.

"So what does he want to do when he leaves school?" The first one asked me.

"Oh, he changes his mind more often than he changes his socks." I replied putting the cups down and beckoning them to take a seat.

"What do you reckon Eric?" I asked. "You've probably got a better idea than I have."

He chuckled softly. "I think we need to get him to go to sixth form first. He's adamant that he doesn't want to go but I'm sure it's the right move. How about you Claire?"

I nodded. "Try convincing him of that though."

"Boy's eh?" The first one shook his head.

"Do you have sons...eh; sorry what's your name?" I asked.

"Clive. Yes, I have seven boys, quite a handful I can tell you."

Yikes, I couldn't imagine having seven boys. One was bad enough. As I went to get a gulp of tea I realised that Eric was starting to look at me strangely.

"Is everything okay Eric?" I asked.

"Oh yes, it's just that when I came in I assumed... Sorry what was your name...Clive? I assumed Clive was your husband. I was just a bit taken aback when you asked his name. Sorry, like they say never assume." He paused. "I'm sorry to interrupt, but may I use your *facilities*?"

"It's through there." I said pointing.

As soon as he was gone I turned to Clive. "So you two don't know each other?"

He looked at me and shook his head. "Up until Eric said that, I thought he was your husband."

"But…you are one of my son's teachers?"

"No Madam, I'm with the church of the latter day saints. I was just hoping to bring you the word of God on this fine morning." He bent down and opened his briefcase to get his pamphlets out.

Oh no, Mormons!

"I don't need any pamphlets, I've already got some. Look I don't mean to be rude but there's been a misunderstanding. When I invited you in I thought you were my son's teacher. I'm really sorry but you'll have to leave."

"Oh." He said, looking morosely down into his tea cup. "It's just so rare to be invited in for tea. Do you think maybe I could finish it before I go?" He asked me so hopefully I really couldn't say no.

Jesus Christ this was all I needed. But, the absolute last thing I wanted to do was to make a scene in front of my son's teacher. I'd have to bite the bullet and pretend that I had invited Clive in on purpose. Otherwise how much of an idiot would I look?

I turned to him with gritted teeth. "Can you just sit quietly though while Eric and I discuss my son's future?"

"Oh, absolutely. You won't even know I'm here."

He beamed.

To Eric's credit, he was very patient while Clive was going on and on and *on*. Poor Eric obviously thought that we must be a family of Mormons. He didn't even finish his tea that I noted was still half full when he left.

"You really have to go now Clive." I told him as I closed the door behind Eric.

"Okay, I suppose so." He said sadly. "It's very cold outside and it's not pleasant being yelled at by people all day." He sighed pathetically.

"Well, Clive, there's a simple answer to that. Go home and stop bugging people!"

With that, thankfully he left.

I went through to the lounge and gathered up the tea cups, placing them in the sink ready to wash before darting off back to the toilet to throw up. After I'd finished being sick and washed my face I cringed as I looked in the mirror and realised that when I had lent my head on the fridge earlier to cool down it had left the indentation of the word 'tit' on my forehead. "Oh no!" I cried in horror as I realised I had just sat through an interview with 'tit' on my forehead. What the hell would Paul's teacher have thought? That I'm a Mormon with the word 'tit' on my forehead? Why 'tit'? Couldn't it have been 'Volvo'?

As I rubbed frantically at my forehead I heard the doorbell go again. "God now what?" I yelled as I flung the door open expecting it to be Clive whining again. It wasn't. An older gentleman in a tweed coat was staring at the pink knickers that I had forgotten to remove from the rose bush.

"Sorry about that." I said snatching them up and hiding them behind my back. "Can I help you with something?"

"Yes, I think so." He flustered. "A colleague called me earlier and told me you seemed very interested in joining our faith? So here I am with some pamphlets for you." He smiled sweetly.

Chapter Eleven

The following day I had a brainwave. Today I would stop all of the nuisance religious nutters from knocking on my door once and for all! I was immensely proud of my ingenious plan and hopped onto the bus with a spring in my step. Spotting the old lady that had been kind enough to invite me for tea; I waved and made my way over to her. "Hello Violet, how are you?"

She smiled and moved her shopping bags so that I could sit next to her. "I'm fine thank you Dear, how are you?"

Good question.

"I'm okay thanks. Much better than last time I saw you anyway."

"Oh that's good. I must admit I have been a little worried about you. You certainly had a lot on your plate last time I saw you." She peered at me out of her horn-rimmed glasses with concern.

I cringed. "Yeah I'm really sorry about that, it was the day from hell."

"Oh that's okay lovey, you know where I am anytime you need to chat."

I was touched. "That's really sweet of you Violet

thank you."

We lapsed into a companionable silence for a while before Violet asked, "So what are you up to today then?"

I turned around in my seat to face her with a beam on my face. "I think I've thought of a way to stop the God-bothers from...well, bothering me."

"Oh yes?" She asked looking a little baffled.

"I'm going to fight fire with fire." I said with my best mischievous look.

"Sounds intriguing." She chuckled. "Tell me all about it."

*****

I returned home with smug look on my face according to TLS. He was sat on the kitchen counter eating monster-munch and getting crumbs all over his school jumper.

"Oh I'm just having a good day." I told his scowling face.

"I haven't." He said crossing his arms indignantly. "Today I got told by my careers teacher that our family has converted to Moronism. What the hell is he on about? We don't believe in any of that crap. Where's he got that idea from?"

Feeling the little tick starting in my left eye, I held my breath and counted to ten.

"Okay, first of all it isn't *Moronism* you moron it's *Mormonism*. And no, we haven't converted, it was just a misunderstanding."

He pulled a face at me which I didn't care for.

"It's all these God-botherers coming here every week that are to blame. They won't go away and they won't take no for an answer. So anyway, I have a plan to get rid of them forever." I said with a smile."

He sat back frowning and screwing up his empty crisp packet before sailing it over the top of my head and into the bin behind me. "What plan?"

"Well think about it, in the last six months we've had on our doorstep: - three sets of Jehovah's witnesses, Hara-Krishna's, that strange band of hippy-happy clappers, the local vicar, and now bloody Mormons! And the more I tell them we're atheists the more they seem to see us as a challenge! So, I think if they all believe we're already religious they might stop pestering us and leave us alone."

He raised his eyebrows with curiosity. "So what do you have in mind?"

"This!" I said pulling from my bag the lovely brass menorah I had bought in town.

He took it from my hands looking puzzled. "A candle-stick, what good is that?"

"It's a Jewish menorah. If we put it in our front-room-window the God-botherers will see it and leave us alone." I grinned at the simplicity of it.

"Hang on a minute, doesn't that just mean that we'll get Jewish people knocking on the door instead?"

"No." I scoffed. "Jewish people never go knocking

on people's doors bugging them to convert. Trust me, this'll work."

He didn't look convinced but humoured me by putting the menorah in pride of place in the centre of the front room window. He turned back to me with a smile. "You know there is another way?"

"Oh yes?"

"We could always put an upside down cross in the window and let them think we're devil worshippers."

"Well you do have the horns." I conceded. "But I think we'll keep that for plan B."

He carried on looking out of the net curtains for a minute before grunting "At last!"

"At last what?" I asked.

"Jenny's here, I'll go let her in and then we're off upstairs to do homework."

I bet that was what they'd be doing.

"Hi Claire." She smirked from the hallway as I heard the door bang closed behind her.

"Yes, hello." I grimaced back, trying not to stare with annoyance at her red bra-strap that was hanging half way down her arm.

She popped her chewing gum while narrowing her eyes at me and smirked as she followed my son up the stairs.

'Please God don't let them get married.' I begged the God I don't believe in.

***

The therapist interrupted me again. To be honest she didn't look very well. The pulsing vein in her forehead would probably rival mine.

"Am I annoying you?" I asked tentatively.

"Of course not, I'm a professional I don't get annoyed with a patient." She said, sounding annoyed. "I'm simply trying to understand this fixation on religion." She cleared her throat before continuing. "From what you've been telling me it's obvious that you have problems with faith, as well as the fear of possibly being a bigot, and of course your family 'issues'. But where does this problem with religion come from? You've made it quite clear that you're an atheist. So why do you spend such a lot of time thinking about something that annoys you so much?"

She had a point.

"In my defence, I wouldn't have a problem with religion if people would stop trying to convert me all the time. I honestly believe in live-and-let-live, and if people want to believe in their magic invisible friend that is fine with me. But just don't expect me to go along with the delusion. *And,* don't come knocking on my door, coming into my house under false pretences in an effort to try and corrupt me." I was starting to get annoyed now and I could hear my voice getting louder.

The therapist looked like she was biting her tongue and she was flicking her pen on and off furiously. My leg was starting to twitch in time with it.

"Some people find religion a...comfort." She said through gritted teeth.

It was at that point that my eyes fell on the little gold crucifix around her neck. 'Oh shit,' I thought, 'she's one of them.' Now I was even more annoyed.

I fought to hold my temper as I replied. "I agree. People *do* seek comfort in religion, in much the same way children seek the comfort of Father Christmas."

"I find that very offensive." She snapped, dropping her therapist hat. Gone was the professional, here was the woman, and she was pissed off.

"I'm sorry but I think it's the perfect parallel." I said rising to my feet. "God knows when you've been naughty; he knows when you've been nice? Well that sounds remarkably familiar."

Something in me snapped as I leapt up onto my plastic chair, and before she could yell... "Get the syringe..." I had launched into my own special version of my favourite Christmas carol. I pointed at her as I began to sing at the top of my lungs.

"You better watch out
You better not cry
You better not pout
I'm telling you why
Jesus Christ is coming to town.

He sees you when you're weeing
He knows when you're half-baked
He knows you've screwed the choir boy

So don't get caught for goodness sake!"

I started to clap along with myself as I was really on a roll.

"He's got a big beard
And probably wears tights;
He's gonna find out
Who gave him pubic lice.
Jesus Christ is coming to town"

Before I could think of another chorus I was dragged down from my pedestal both figuratively and literally as I was carted off back to my room to 'cool off'.

Chapter Twelve

"Okay Claire, things got a little heated yesterday. I think we should try and draw a line under it and continue on. A fresh day and a fresh start." The much calmer therapist said.

I was sitting in my chair trying to make myself look as small as possible. I was so ashamed of my behaviour the day before; my outburst was inexcusable. I don't know where the rage came from, and I could barely look in her in the eye as I offered her a meek apology.

"I'm really sorry." I mumbled.

"Apology accepted." She said very business-like. "I'm actually quite pleased that it happened, at least now I've seen an example of your outbursts for myself. It's very helpful really."

"I don't know what came over me; I'm really not the sort of person who gets mad like that."

She looked at me thoughtfully. "Has it ever occurred to you that maybe you should be? Maybe if you voice your annoyance more then it won't build up in you like a pressure cooker."

I could see where she was coming from. "I really don't like making a fuss; normally I can just turn the other cheek and put things away in a little box at the back of my mind where they can't annoy me anymore. But lately...I don't know, it's like the little box in my mind has started to crack and things keep popping out."

The therapist raised her eyebrows and nodded her head before knocking me off my feet with, "How's your sex life?"

"Pardon?" I stammered in surprise and embarrassment.

"How...is...your...sex...life?"

"Fine thank you very much." I said primly crossing my legs.

"Do you have a sex life?" She was sitting forward and peering over her glasses looking far more amused than I was happy with.

I could feel my cheeks flushing as I spluttered out, "I'm a married woman, what do you think?"

"It doesn't matter what I think. It's a simple enough question. Do you have a sex life?"

Why didn't she say it a bit louder? I'm sure there's someone across the road that didn't quite catch what she said. "I'm quite happy in that department thank you."

"So do you and your husband have regular sex?"

The cow was enjoying this. Payback for the Jesus bashing yesterday this was. "Well, my husband has regular sex."

"But not with you?"

"Not with me." I said annoyed.

"Why not with you?"

"Because he's got a tart!" I snapped.

"What came first? The lack of sex or the tart - erm sorry the other woman?"

"Does it matter?" I glared at my slippers.

"It might."

"Fine, we hadn't…'you know what' for a while before he got the tart."

"Why?"

"I don't know, I suppose we just, sort of… got bored of each other. We've been together since school; it got to the point where it got icky."

"Icky?"

"You know, like if your cousin went to give you a kiss or something. You know, icky."

She shook her head at me again. I know she was irritated. "So he got 'the other woman', I'm sorry I just don't like the word tart. It makes the feminist in me go crazy." She threw her hands in the air shuddering. "So, he got 'the other woman' and what did you get?"

"A Sudoku book and a twitch."

She rubbed her eyes in frustration. I had annoyed her with my honesty again. See, this is why it's much better to keep your mouth shut.

"Do you ever wonder if maybe you are sexually repressed?"

I have always had a nervous laugh when I feel uncomfortable and in this situation I had never felt more uncomfortable in my life, and that included the time I had to put a condom on a banana in sex education and laughed hysterically until I was sent out. Now, all I wanted to do with the whole of my being was pull my jumper over my face and smirk.

I think my reluctance must've been obvious, as my therapist said: - "Never mind, we'll come back to this later. Carry on with your story. It's not like either of us has a home to go to or anything." She then pointedly looked at her watch sighing.

Sarcasm? Not very professional in my opinion.

Putting her head in her hands she asked, "Tell me what happened when you put the Menorah in your front window."

***

The following Sunday was wonderful, I saw the happy-clappers all congregating at the entrance to my street as usual, but not one of them knocked on my door. As I got up to make a cup of tea I saw one older lady open my garden gate and start to set off up my path with a determined look on her face when she suddenly stopped in her tracks and stared at my front room window before pointing her head-scarf in the opposite direction and making a hasty retreat.

I was jumping for joy behind the net curtains shouting "YES! Have it you gits!" It had worked. I was a genius! With a bit of luck, I should be bible-basher free from now on. I watched in delight as I saw the woman outside exit my garden gate and flick the catch up on Mr and Mrs Little's gate next door. Hm, I thought, I better remember to ask them if they want a menorah for Christmas.

If I could just get rid of the double glazing salesmen and the cold-callers next I could die a happy woman.

With a beam I altered the fridge magnets from 'penis' to 'denis' by pivoting the 'P'. Today was a good day, I thought. What is it people say? Today is the first day of the rest of my life!

***

Monday though brought me back down to earth with a bump. I was just coming out of the bakery from where I was sacked, after going in to pay the bill for the leftovers I had arranged for Jean the homeless lady when the shit hit that fan. I had gone in there during my former boss's dinner break as I obviously didn't want to bump into her, and after paying my former colleague, I made a hasty retreat. I was startled as I was tapped on the shoulder by a vaguely familiar lady who I believed lived down the road from me. The glamorous lady -who was around the same age as me but definitely faring better than I was- smiled at me sweetly as she spoke. "Hi there, I'm sorry to bother you. Claire isn't it?"

"Yes." I replied nervously, wondering what the hell she wanted from me.

"I'm Fiona; I live just down the road from you

at number thirty-two. I *just* realised that you're Jewish! I didn't realise there were any other Jewish families in the area, I'm sorry I haven't spoken to you before but I had no idea you were Jewish too."

I was staring at her like a rabbit in the headlights, my brain stuttering trying to come up with something, anything that I could offer as an explanation that wouldn't come out sounding anti-Semitic, or make me look like a moron.

Before I had a chance to utter a single word I heard another voice over my shoulder.

"Mrs Porter? Claire?"

I turned and felt my stomach drop as I saw to my horror that it was Eric, my son's careers teacher.

"Oh, hello." I said, feeling the colour drain from my face.

"I'm sorry I left in such a hurry the other day. I'm afraid it was a little rude of me. It's just that, as an atheist I've never been that comfortable discussing religion in quite so much depth. Colin was a little...full on for what I'm used to." He pulled a sheepish face. "Again, I'm really very sorry that I was so rude."

"Oh, don't worry, it's quite alright. I'm a little... new to religion too." I said looking from Eric who believed I was a Mormon -to Fiona who believed I was Jewish. 'Please,' I thought, 'let the ground open up and swallow me right now! I promise, if a hole appeared in the pavement right now I would happily skip into it.'

Fiona was smiling at Eric sympathetically. "It's understandable, our religion isn't for everyone. But it wouldn't do for us all to be the same would it?"

Eric looked very relieved at having been let off the hook. I, however, was having an internal meltdown. How did I manage to get myself into this mess? I am a bloody atheist! I couldn't just blurt that out though, how on earth could I explain about the accidental Mormon in my living room and the not so accidental 'I'm Jewish' flashing neon sign in my front room window? I was about to fake a heart attack when Fiona started speaking to me, distracting me from rubbing my left arm in readiness to drop to the pavement.

"Actually Claire, speaking of religion, my family's having a celebration next Saturday and I wondered if you and your family would like to come?"

"Next Saturday?" God brain, think! Come up with an excuse, something, anything! I was completely blank. "Yes, that would be nice, why not." The voice said, that came out from my face.

"Sorry Claire I better leave you to it, I just popped out of class on my dinner break. Best get back." Eric said lifting up his bag of sausage rolls for effect.

"Bye." I called after him, thinking 'take me with you, I'm an atheist too'.

Chapter Thirteen

So apparently, the following Saturday I would be going to my first Bah Mitzvah! I had tried to explain myself to Max and Paul about how it was all just a big mix-up, but Paul just snorted and laughed at me, something along the lines of 'serves you right for making everyone at school think I'm a moron.'

"MORMON you moron!" I snapped back at him.

"Whatever!" He shrugged, and went through to the front room dropping down onto the sofa with a bang before flicking MTV on at a level that was making me twitch.

Max was staring at me with thinly disguised amusement. "Normal people don't get themselves into situations like this you know."

"Please come with me?" I begged. "I can't go on my own; I don't know what to do."

"You got yourself into this you can get yourself out of it."

He was enjoying this, I could tell from the way his shoulders were shaking as he put the milk away in the fridge.

"But what do I *do* at a Bah mitzvah? Do I have

to say anything? Is there anything I'm supposed to take? God what do I wear?" I was really starting to freak out.

Max pulled his shaking shoulders from out of the fridge and turned to me grinning. "Look, stop being stupid, just go see the woman and tell her it's been a big misunderstanding. She'll probably think it's funny. I know I do."

"I can't do that. She'll think I'm a complete nut job. Plus, she's gonna ask why the man I was talking to was speaking to me about how religious I am. What do I say then? Oh it's okay he's just under the impression that I'm a moron. I mean *Mormon*!" I pulled my head down to rest on the counter-top in a sulk.

Max came up behind me and rested his hands on my shoulders, quite tenderly I thought. For a brief moment I let myself enjoy it before slamming the door in my head locking him and the tart out. I stiffened and shrugged out of his grip. He sat down on the stool next to me with a sigh. "You know what? I'll go see her for you if you like. I'll tell her you've been under a bit of pressure lately and the situation with God-botherers has driven you to... well...stupid measures."

"Would you really go see her?" I asked meekly. "What if she thinks I'm an idiot?"

He smiled shaking his head. "What was it Forrest Gump said? Stupid is as stupid does."

Arsehole, I thought.

"What number does she live at?"

"Number thirty-two I think she said."

"Okay, I'll go get this over and done with then," he said with a resigned sigh.

"Thank you." I called after him before the door bumped closed.

There was a part of me that was regretting sending Max to explain my stupidity already. Surely it would be better just to go to the blasted thing and grin and bear it for a few hours. That would probably be far less stressful than accidently offending the local Jewish community wouldn't it?

I sat with my stomach in knots for the entire half-hour that Max was gone. I looked at the kitchen clock for the umpteenth time. What was taking him so long? I got up and peered through the edge of the kitchen window and then shit myself as I found myself face to face with Mr Little from next-door again.

"Everything okay Mr Little?" I mouthed.

"Fine thank you. How are you?"

"I'm fine, thank you."

He continued to stare at me grinning.

"Why are you looking in my window Mr Little?"

"Just wanted to know if you were in yet?"

"Well, here I am!" I declared with annoyance.

"Good, good to know." With that, he doffed his wig at me and departed with a wink.

What the hell was that about? I wondered. My next-door-neighbours have always been a little strange but this was taking the biscuit!

By the time Max came back ten minutes later I was frantic. What the hell could possibly be taking him so long? Was he having a fight? Was he defending my honour? More likely he was having a really good laugh at my expense. I thought with a huff.

He came in through the back door and proceeded to take his shoes off while ignoring me.

"Well?" I asked.

"Oh, sorry." He said turning around. "I went to number thirty-two but they didn't know what I was talking about. Apparently they're Roman-Catholics. So I asked if they knew if any of their neighbours was called Fiona and they said they'd never heard of her." He stood up with a shrug and hung his coat on the back of a stool.

My stomach sank even further. "I'm sure she said number thirty-two!"

"Maybe number thirty-two in a different street, but certainly not this one."

"Oh." I said sitting back down before my legs gave way. "So I can't even cancel it then. I really have to go." I felt my lip start to wobble, so I bit it before sitting up with a start. "Hey, if you haven't been stuck explaining how stupid I am for the last hour where the hell have you been? I've been sat here worried sick!"

"Pub."

"Pub?" I spat.

"Just a quick half as I was passing."

"Brilliant, just brilliant." I seethed before sloping off to furiously wash my windows. I was chuntering away to myself under my breath about the futility of it all. Here I was stuck in a house I hate with a husband who doesn't care about me, a son who doesn't respect me, I'm now unemployable, my neighbours like to spy on me and despite being a Godless heathen I now belong to two different religions! I might as well just cut my losses, grow my hair and join a cult!

As I was scrubbing the bottom half of my front room window I spotted a BT open reach van across the road. I stood bolt upright with my chin in the air and marched out of the door to accost the BT engineer.

"Oi! You! You there!" I steamed across the road. "Are you here to fix my phone lines?"

The startled engineer took a step back up into his van as I grabbed the door and flung it wide open.

"What?" He looked a little nervous of me.

"ARE YOU HERE TO FIX MY PHONE LINE?" As well as my now familiar twitch in my eye I could also feel my nose twitching. "You cut me off more than a week ago!"

"I'm sorry; this is my first day I wasn't here last week." He lied.

"Oh, so there are two BT engineers working in my street with purple Mohawks are there?"

He tried to get the van door out of my hands and lock himself in the van...but I was having none of it.

"FIX MY PHONE LINE!" I roared as I fought to keep hold of the door.

"Go away!" He said in a panic. "I don't have to deal with abusing customers. We had a seminar about it and everything."

"Get back out here and fix my phone!" I stumbled back a bit as I lost my grip on the door as he finally slammed it shut and started the engine.

"Oh no you don't!" I had really lost the plot by this time. So I leaped up on the bonnet and pulled myself up by his roof-rack until I was eyeball to eyeball with him through the windscreen. "FIX MY PHONE LINE!" I roared.

His panicked response was to switch on his windscreen wipers. We stared at each other in silence as the washer blades rose and fell between us. It was a brief moment of calm before the storm hit.

I broke the calm as I finally screamed, "AGHHH-HHHH!" and snapped the windscreen wipers off.

"You're bleeding nuts!" He mouthed through the glass before upping his game and turning the screen washer on me.

"Ugh!" I shook my head at the freezing cold water that had hit me in the face.

He started his engine and said, "You've got till the count of three, then I'm putting my foot down whether you're on the bonnet or not!"

By the time he got to three I had grabbed the roof rack again and hoisted myself onto the roof, clinging on for dear life as he floored the van up my street. From that point on my memory is a little hazy, but I was assured by Max who eventually heard the commotion and came out to drag me off the van, that the last thing I had been shouting from the roof of the van was "I NEED MY PHONE LINES TO GOOGLE BAH MITZVAHS!"

Chapter Fourteen

"This has got to stop!" Max said quietly to me as he dabbed TCP onto the cuts on my palms. "It cost me three-hundred quid to stop that fella going straight to the police. What the hell was going through your mind?"

I winced as the TCP stung my wounds. I felt like I was going to have a heart attack the way the adrenalin was still roaring through my veins. I shrugged at Max as I couldn't find the words.

"There's something seriously wrong with you Claire. I feel like I barely even know you anymore."

"That's rich coming from you." I snapped back.

"What the hell's that supposed to mean?"

"You certainly aren't the man I married. I don't remember there being a tart standing next to us at the altar."

He rubbed his eyes sighing. "Do you *really* want to talk about it? I thought we were happy feigning ignorance."

"Happy?" I said incredulously. "You think we're happy?"

"Well we get by don't we? We have a nice house, a lovely...well, a son." He pulled a wry face, I'm sure he was thinking about Paul's horns. "We get on for the most part don't we? We don't argue as much as most people seem to."

"Maybe that's part of the problem." I countered. "Maybe we just don't care enough to argue with each other." I paused. "Do you think maybe it's time to think about maybe...you know...divorce or something?"

"We can't do that to Paul."

"He's tough, I'm sure he'd handle it fine."

"No, once he's gone off to university or something, then we'll think about where we go from there. Claire, we're both from divorced families. Do you remember how hard it was growing up in a war zone? The tug of war from one parent to the next? Always feeling guilty like it was our fault. Do you remember that Claire cause I sure as hell do."

He had a point, we did both have a really hard time of it when our parents when through their divorces. Mine went through it when I was ten; Max's when he was fourteen. Did we really want to put Paul through that? "I suppose it would be bad timing with this being his last year in high school, and exams and then starting sixth form..."

"See." Max said a little softer. "What's the harm in waiting a couple of years?" He held my hand in the way that used to make me melt; now it just made me want to trap it in a door. "Am I really that hard to live with for just a little while longer?"

I forced a grimace that he mistook for a smile.

"There you go." He preened. "Now what's for tea I'm starving?"

∗∗∗

As I lay in the bath later that night with a flannel covering my eyes, I listened to the self-help cd that Max had 'thoughtfully' brought home with him for me to listen to. The cd cover had advised me to have a relaxing bubble bath with scented candles and to try and relax as I listened to the 'soothing voice' of the narrator. It didn't quite go that way. I couldn't find a scented candle anywhere in the house so I made do with six birthday-cake-candles stuck in a bar of soap, and as for bubble bath –let's just say that I've now run out of fairy liquid.

I found it ironic that a cd aimed at depressed people advocated having an electrical appliance in the bathroom with them. I looked at the CD player perched on the toilet thoughtfully, maybe that could be my plan B?

I lay there for a while listening to the so-called *soothing voice* of the narrator before it dawned on me that he sounded like Alan Partridge. I was laid in a bath of fairy liquid by the light of six birth-day candles wedged in a bar of soap whilst listening to Alan Partridge tell me to *relax*! Once I had the image in my head of Alan Partridge sitting on my toilet in place of the cd player, all thoughts of relaxing were gone. With my eyes closed I could really believe he was sat there on the toilet with his legs crossed looking at me with a condescending expression and disapproving of the mildew on the bathroom ceiling. With a sigh I used my big toe to pull the plug and blew the soap of candles out. Maybe some people just weren't meant to relax?

I was just drying myself on a towel when TLS pounded on the door. "Internet's back on!"

"Mine!" I shouted in a panic trying to get my dressing-gown on despite how wet my skin still was. "Don't go near that computer Paul." I yelled. "It's mine 'till I know what a bah mitzvah is!"

"Too late!" He yelled back. "You snooze you lose!"

"Shit," I chuntered to myself.

I was just tying my hair up into a turban when my phone buzzed to say that I had a text. Swiping the fogged up screen I saw it was from Stephanie. Funny, I thought, I didn't even remember putting her number in my phone.

Emma's having a hen night Friday night.
R u coming?

God, I thought reading the text, hen nights scare the crap out of me. All those drunken women doing stupid dares and wearing L-plates. Plus, all of the strange men following the drunken women about. Although, on the other hand, I did have a great time last time we all went out. But what would Max say? Actually, to hell with Max. Maybe I should go. If nothing else, it might annoy him. Before I had chance to change my mind I decided to be brave and accept.

Ok. Why Not?

Barely ten seconds past before I got a reply.

It's gonna be a blast. Got some great stunts planned!

Oh shit, I thought. I quickly sent my reply.

I'm not doing daft dares

And I don't want any strange men perving at me.

I just wanted to get that clear from the start. I've only ever been on one hen night before and it scared the crap out of me. Stephanie took a while before she replied to me this time and I was starting to think that maybe I'd been a bit too blunt with my last text. It was around an hour later when she sent this: -

Understood. We've got a fool proof plan to make sure no man's going to bother you! lol.

I didn't care for the 'lol' on the end. What the hell was the plan?

***

Once I finally got near the laptop I was pleasantly surprised to find that I wouldn't have to do anything special in preparation for the bah mitzvah. Apparently a gift or money was the only thing I'd need to take. No special hat was needed for me thank goodness. Paul had tried to convince me that I would need to wear a skull cap but I knew that couldn't be right, and despite his protests to the contrary, I knew for a fact I wouldn't have to be carried about the room on a special chair. So with my mind temporarily at rest about the whole thing I decided to try and put it out of my mind until the day. I had an outfit picked out in readiness so there was nothing to really think about until the day. So now *that* worry was out of my brain it was time to worry about something else for a while.

As I lay in bed I pondered what order I should start worrying about things again. My sham of a marriage? Maybe the fact that I can't get a job? How about my lack of mental health, that's always good for a laugh these days? I honestly don't understand how my life turned out to be so shit. I've always done my best to me a nice person, I've never hurt anyone and I've always gone the extra mile to help other people. I married for love not convenience, and I *really* have tried to make it work, but now's it's got to the point of...no point at all really. It doesn't seem like five minutes since I was Paul's age, staring bravely back at the world that I believed was mine for the taking. Why did nobody mention to me that while I was busy taking care of everyone else that I was getting old and as Paul puts it 'past it'? How did it happen? When did it happen? And more importantly what the hell am I going to do now?

I lay awake all night listening to the clock on the landing strike every hour, thinking to myself every time it began to gong –there's another hour of my life gone, and another, and another...

Beside me Max slept like a baby beside me with a stupid smile on his face.

Chapter Fifteen

"Mum please…" I tried to get a word in as she was lecturing me down the phone.

"Claire if you don't come and visit me soon I'm cutting you off. See, this is what you've driven me to, I have to threaten my only daughter in order to get her to visit me."

I stuck my tongue out at the phone. "I haven't had chance to come and see you Mum, I've been busy. Hey what do you mean I'm your only daughter, what about Rachel?"

"I'm not speaking to her until she gets rid of that boyfriend of hers."

"What boyfriend? I didn't know she had one." It was news to me, but then again my sister and I weren't very close.

"Huh." She said with a snotty tone. "He's bloody Polish. He can barely speak a word of English, not that I can understand anyway. I've told her it's him or me. Well, let's just say, she's made her bed now she'll just have to bloody well lie in it. She's out of the will anyway."

I took it she'd told our mother where to go. Good for her. "Look Mum, I have to go, but I promise I'll come and see you next week." I crossed my fingers behind my back.

"I'll believe it when I see it." She said before hanging up.

To think I had been looking forward to having a phone line again! I wish I could say that was the only annoying call that I got that day, but no. Later on, I was just finishing filling in a job application form for a telesales job when I was disturbed by the phone.

"Hello?" I answered.

"Good morning! May I speak to Mrs Porter please?" The slightly Chinese sounding man asked me. I was already suspecting this was probably another con but after the 'Bobert incident' I didn't want to jump to any conclusions.

"Yes that's me."

"How are you this fine morning?" He sounded very happy, I'd give him that.

"I'm fine thank you." I said through gritted teeth. "But I don't want to buy anything."

"And I'm not trying to sell you anything Mrs Porter. I am simply calling to tell you about our great discounts that we have here at *Green Glazing Company.* It doesn't matter if you're struggling with finances in today's economy; we have finance options for everyone's budget!"

I put the phone down with a bang before a thought occurred to me. This company have called me up several times to pester me about double glazing, I wondered if I could use the same lateral thinking as I did on the religious front? *Yes,* I might be accidently attending a bah mitzvah on Saturday *but* my menorah had stopped the rest of the god-botherers from bugging me. Yes, I was sure there was some affirmative action that could be taken here. I dialled 1471 and got the number of the glazing company that had just bothered me. I entered the number into my phonebook as 'double bloody glazing'. There, at least next time they rang I'd recognise the caller.

The following day I was delighted to see from my caller ID that it was the same glazing company again. "Got you now you buggers!" I sniggered before picking the phone up and in my best Asian/Welsh accent said: - "Good morning, this is Porters Glazing company. How can I be helping you today?"

Silence at the other end of the line.

"I am sorry, is there someone wanting to buy some best quality double glazing? Don't be shy, I won't bite. That costs extra, but I do have fantastic finance options." I grinned to myself. My accent was sounding much like Apu off *The Simpsons.*

I heard the click as someone put the phone down without speaking.

"Ha!" I put the phone down with a bang before shouting. "One-nil!"

I decided there and then that I was going to fight fire with fire. I could maybe even think of it as a type of therapy. It had certainly cheered me up and had stopped me from blowing a gasket like I had been doing of late. Hell, it was a while since I'd had a hobby.

I flicked through the yellow pages until I found the number of the company who ring me up every week asking me to 'just do a short survey' that lasts on average around an hour, where they seem to want to know everything about me bar the colour of my knickers. (Actually one man asked what colour knickers I had on but I'm not certain he was actually from a survey company.) Usually at the end of one of these endless surveys they try to get me to buy particular brand of washing powder or something. It's very annoying.

I giggled to myself as I dialled their number.

"Hello, you're through to Lorraine at LGP how may I help?" The polite sing/song voice said.

"Hello Lorraine," I gushed, "so nice to speak to you, how are you?" This was fun.

"I'm fine thank you for asking." She sounded a little wary though I thought. "Who am I speaking to please?"

"Bobert." I replied.

"Excuse me, I didn't catch that?"

"Bobert." I repeated.

"Ah, yes. What can I do for you today?" She sounded a little puzzled.

"I just want to ask you a few questions if I may? I have had quite a few dealings with your company in the last few months and I wondered if I could ask you to complete a short survey for me over the phone?"

"Oh. Well, yes, sure that would be okay. What would you like to ask me?"

I thought for a moment. "Mm, when was your company established?"

I could hear her humming to herself. "Let me see, I believe that was back in 1992."

"Great thanks." I pretended I was writing that down. "And how many people are employed at your firm?"

"I'm not sure about overall, but in this building there's around twenty of us."

"Just one last question if I may."

"Of course." She said pleasantly.

"What colour are your knickers!"

Click, as the phone went dead. I laughed to myself, whoever thought I would be a pervert caller?

***

"You're in a good mood." Paul observed when he came in later that night.

I had been alternating all day between despair at my outburst and subsequent attack of the BT man, and elation at getting one over on the pesky cold-callers. Paul though, happened to catch me on the highest point of my emotional seesaw.

"Just had a better day today that's all." I told him briefly going to pat him on the head before changing my mind as I observed how much hair-spray he had going on there. My hand hovered over the sticky mass not quite wanting to touch it. "You know you really ought to use a better hairspray." I told him. "If you insist on such a stupid hair-cut you ought to at least try and do something better with it."

"Back off woman!" He said holding his fingers up at me like a cross. "My hair is my own."

"I was only trying to help." I sulked.

"Well thanks but no thanks."

I sighed. "What happened to my little boy? You were so cute when you were little. Do you remember that little blue sun hat you used to wear?" I smiled nostalgically before the smile fell from my face as I took in the grumpy teenager with horns and eyeliner that sat frowning before me. "Never mind."

He shook his head at me with a look that I didn't care for. "Anyway," he said, "have you bought a special hat for your bar-whatsit yet?"

"I don't have to wear a special hat, I googled it."

"You do," he lied, "we did all about it in religious education at school. You have to wear one of those little cap things and I'm sure you have to wear two different coloured socks."

"Piss of Paul!"

"Maybe not the socks thing but you defo have to wear your pants inside out."

"Leave me alone." I said resting my chin on the

counter top with a bang.

"Oh come on Mum it *is* funny."

"If you think it's so funny you can bloody well come with me."

"I've told you I can't; I've got a football match on. But let me know next time you get roped into a religious do, I'll defo be up for it next time. Can you try and make it a Buddhist thing next time? There's an orange sheet in my room that'll look great on you."

Chapter Sixteen

Before I knew it the week had rolled around to Friday and the dreaded hen-do. I was right about it annoying Max, he never actually said anything but I think the way he was grating his teeth as I came down the stairs in my new mini-dress said it all.

"What do you think?" I asked, giving him a twirl.

"To the belt?" Came the sarcastic reply.

I must admit I was surprised how well I had scrubbed up. I had about an inch worth of concealer on my eye-bags which made me look much less tired than usual, and with a bit of lippy and a decent blow-dry to my mane I didn't look too bad.

Max was looking me up and down disapprovingly from head to foot before his eyes came to rest on my bust. "They're new!" He commented.

I was a little self-conscious about my cleavage. I had bought a 'two sizes' bigger bra to help fill my dress out a bit, but it seemed preposterous to me how much casing my two little fried eggs had wrapped around them now. I felt like I was wearing a pair of false boobs from a joke shop. Kenny Everett! That was who I felt like- when he used to put that big frilly frock on.

I found myself slouching a little to hide my new Kenny Everetts.

"What time will you be back?" He asked me curtly. He was still looking at my breasts with puzzlement.

"Don't know." I said with a flick of my hip as I headed out the door. "Don't wait up!"

***

"Here she is!" The group of girls waiting for me announced as I joined the queue outside of the club. There must've been around twenty of them, most of whom I didn't know from Adam, but I recognised the 'hen' Emma, Stephanie and Carly. The poor hen was dressed up with the stupid L plates and veil that I had expected, and the rest of them were wearing short white crop-tops with silly slogans topped off with silly pink-deely-boppers on their heads. I suddenly felt very over-dressed and wriggled in my 'belt' self-consciously.

"Don't worry," Stephanie said with an evil grin, "you've got a t-shirt too."

I didn't care for the smirk she was exchanging with Carly. I caught a glimpse of a few of the t-shirts as the girls milled about in the queue. One said *'Don't just stare at my tits, buy me a drink!'* Another said, *'I like your jeans can I try the zipper?'* Stephanie proudly stretched her t-shirt out so that I could read her slogan, *'I don't care if you have small boobs, I still wanna see em!'*

"Good one." I told her uncomfortably wondering if she had my own in mind.

"I know right?" She beamed. "Check out Carly's. Hey Carly," she yelled. "Show Claire your T-shirt!"

Carly turned around with a grin so I could read hers. *'I'll let you play with mine if you let me play with yours!'*

"Classy." I nodded with a smile. Inside, I was terrified. It was turning out to be everything I had ever dreaded about hen nights.

"Are you ready to see yours?" Stephanie asked with a giggle.

"Oh, as ready as I'll ever be." Oh God they've got one for me! Please let this night be over with soon.

She dove into the plastic bag that she had been holding onto. "Okay, now you know you said you didn't want any weird men perving at you or hitting on you? Well, I think we have the perfect T-shirt for you."

I almost died on the spot as I read the slogan of the T-shirt I would be wearing for the evening. *'Back off...I have chlamydia'.*

I looked up at their grinning faces in horror.

"See!" Stephanie said proudly. "You won't have *any* bother on that front!"

Oh my God! They expected me to wear *that*? All night? In public? They were looking at me expectantly, so what could I do? I peeled my white cotton cardigan off briefly revealing my Kenny Everetts before pulling the T-shirt over the top of them.

"There you go!" Carly and Stephanie laughed. "Now let's get inside and get a good seat at the front before the strippers come in."

"Look at Claire's face!" Stephanie said cooing.

"What's wrong Claire?" Carly asked laughing at my discomfort.

"I know what's wrong." Stephanie said kindly.

I looked up at her hopefully. Was she going to let me off the hook? Would she take this dreaded t-shirt from me and throw it away?

"She's upset that she doesn't have deely-boppers like we do."

"Aw Hun, you can have mine." Carly said pulling the shocking pink glittery pom-poms from her head and wedging them on the top of my head. "There you go sweetie."

"Thank you." I grimaced back.

I wanted to cry as they linked arms with me and led me inside, feeling the giant pink balls bobbing on my head and clutching my cardigan for dear life – waiting for the opportunity to put it back on and hide my chlamydia shame!

***

"I don't like the way that stripper keeps thrusting himself in my direction." I said to Carly as we queued up at the bar. I could see him still looking over at me, half dressed as a cowboy and cocking his hat at me.

"I think he's got his eye on you." She said with

a toss of her brown locks. The Tina Turner wig had gone tonight; tonight she was more 'rocking the Beyonce' as she put it. I felt positively nun-like standing next to her, that is if a nun were ever accused of having an STD. I pulled at my annoying T-shirt with a frown.

The barman did a double take at Carly as she waved her £20 note at him. He shook his head bewildered before plastering a smile on his face. "So what are you ladies drinking?" He asked with a cheeky wink.

"Sex on the beach for me...if you're not busy?" Carly bellowed across the bar suggestively.

He laughed before turning to me and raising his eyebrows quizzically.

"Oh, erm, I don't know." I had a Bar mitzvah to get up for in the morning. "Just orange juice please."

"Pardon love?" He shouted over the noise.

Carly answered for me. "She said she wants a Knee Trembler."

"No I didn't..."

She shushed me and carried on as if I wasn't there.

"What's that love?" The barman asked. "That's not one I know."

"I'd love to show you." She said grinning. "Okay, it's Passoa, vodka and fresh orange juice."

"I don't want anything strong." I hissed at her.

"Trust me you'll love it."

She was right, I did. That one and the next five.

***

"Claire, Claire, Claire!" The crowd clapped as I as I licked the whipped-cream off the stripper's nipple. He seemed to be getting some unnecessary job satisfaction from his work as he sprayed the remainder of the cream onto his unmentionables.

"Oh no Pal." I said looking down and backing off. "I'm not a pervert!" I turned to the baying crowd shaking my hands at them, "No. I'm not a pervert!"

"Boo!" They hissed at me.

"Tough." I yelled back stumbling down off the stage.

Back on stage the stripper was looking sadly at my departing bottom as it left the stage. He turned to the microphone. "I've never said this before, but can someone please give me Chlamydia back?"

The crowd cheered with many offers.

I sat back down in my seat with a bump. It took a few minutes for the room to stop spinning around me as I tried to concentrate on getting my glass to my lips without poking myself in the eye with the little cocktail umbrella. It took me a moment through my drunken stupor to feel something sticky on my chin. I stuck my tongue out to sample it. "Bloody whipped-cream." I chuntered to myself. "I'd rather have licked it off a cream bun."

***

"Claire." Stephanie hisses through the darkness.

"Claire where the hell are you I can't see a thing."

"Is that you Steph?" I heard Carly patting someone in the dark.

"Hang on," I said, "the lights here somewhere." I was feeling all around my living room wall for the light-switch that was hiding from me. "Oh here it is." I flicked it on flooding my front room with blinding floodlights.

"Ow." Called the two drunks laid out on the floor covering their eyes. "Too bright."

Now that I could see properly I clambered over them to turn on the lamp in the corner which had a much softer glow than the blinding light above us. "Shhh." I told them as I climbed back over them and on unsteady feet made my way across the living room to turn off the bloody awful ceiling light. "Oh that's better." I said leaning against the wall for support. I could see Carly and Stephanie pulling themselves up onto my sofa and sitting back with a huff.

"So this is where Max lives." Slurred Carly, looking around her.

"Should we wake him up?" Stephanie asked me brightly. "Max!" She started to call loudly.

"Sounds like a dog!" Carly observed before the pair of them descended into giggles "Here Max! Here Maxy, Maxy!"

"Shhh." I complained.

Stephanie was laughing and trying to struggle to her feet. "Come on Max, here boy. Come and fetch me something."

I tried once again to get them to shut up. "Look, I've told you can crash here the night but you can't wake Max up."

"Why not?" Carly slurred. "He could make me a sandwich?"

"Yeah!" Stephanie added. "Go on Claire tell him to make us something to eat."

"Wake him up to make us sandwiches? He'd go nuts!"

"So?" Carly added. "What do you care you don't like him anyway."

Hm she wasn't wrong there. I sank down heavily between them to puzzle it out. "Should I make the sandwiches?" I asked them anxiously.

"NO!" They bellowed at the same time.

"Are you sure, 'cause I mean, I *always* make the sandwiches." I repeated it to myself again. "I always make the sandwiches." I felt as if some profound bit of knowledge was being imparted into my brain. "I always make the sandwiches." I whispered.

"Aren't you tired of making the sandwiches?" Steph asked me goadingly.

"Yes?" I didn't sound sure.

Carly joined in. "Hell yes you're tired of making the sandwiches!"

"Hell yes I'm tired of making the sandwiches." I repeated in a timid voice.

"Then say it a bit louder!" Carly said kneeling up a bit higher on my sofa.

145

"I'm tired of making the sandwiches."

"Louder!" They cheered.

"I'm tired of making the sandwiches!"

"Louder!"

"I'M TIRED OF MAKING THE SANDWICHES!"

"So what are you going to do about it?" Stephanie asked.

I struggled drunkenly to my feet. "I'm going to get Max to make me a sandwich."

I clambered over Steph's legs wobbling precariously towards the door.

"And us!" Carly called after me. "Don't forget we want some too."

"Max!" I bellowed up the stairs. "Max!" I paused listening for movement. "Max! I want a sandwich!" I made it to the third step up before sitting down as climbing was just too much hard work. "Max!" I called again. "Max!"

"What the hell is going on?" Max demanding coming out of our bedroom wearing only his boxers and rubbing his eyes. "What the hell are you shouting for?"

"A sandwich." I replied tiredly. All this shouting was tiring me out and making me sleepy.

"What?" He demanded? "Are you drunk?"

I shook my head and waved away all the questions. "I want a sandwich and it's your turn."

"What? What the hell are talking about?"

"I want a sandwich and it's your turn." I tried my best to stand but couldn't, so I compromised by leaning against the wall with as much nonchalance as I could muster.

"Go to bed!" He ordered.

"Make me a sandwich."

"Go to bed. Now!"

"You don't get to tell me what to do anymore... Does he?" I asked turning back to the direction of my lounge.

"No!" They called in unison.

"See." I pointed at Max. "Got my Pussy in there for back up!" I nodded.

"Posse!" Carly corrected from the lounge.

"Who the hell have you got in there?" He said pushing past me into the living room.

"Hi Max." They waved happily from the couch.

"Unbelievable!" He said storming past me back up the stairs.

"Wait, Max!" I called after him.

"What?" He snapped.

"What about my sandwich?"

He shook his head at me and slammed the bedroom door closed behind him.

"Are we getting a sandwich?" Stephanie called hopefully.

"Doubt it!" I slurred from the stairs.

Chapter Seventeen

"Okay," said the therapist stopping me, "what was the significance of the sandwich?"

"What do you mean?"

"Why was it so important that Max made you the sandwich?" She was peering at me over those giant glasses again making me very aware of the clumpy blue mascara magnified around her eyes.

"I don't know really. At the time it made perfect sense, I always made the sandwiches for everyone and no-one *ever* made one for me."

"So what you were saying was that you were tired of looking after other people and you felt that it was time for someone to look after you?"

I nodded. "I suppose so."

"So after your outburst did you feel that you got your 'sandwich'?" She said sandwich with air quotes which I found confusing.

"No, it turned out we'd run out of bread."

She huffed at me again in a derogatory manner that I didn't care for. "Okay, back to the story, what happened next?"

***

I awoke the next morning with a pneumatic drill banging through my brain. At least that was what it felt like. I woke up feeling very confused on the floor of my front room and for some reason I was wrapped up in a rug. I shuffled out of my little cocoon in a panic wondering what the hell had gone on. I peered across the room and saw Stephanie laid out drooling attractively across my armchair before turning startled at Carly who was fast asleep on my couch. At some point in the night Carly had taken the Beyonce wig off and placed it on the top of my pot poodle statue. The little pot pouch looked quite funny donning a Beyonce wig, but it was Carly that I couldn't stop staring at. Although her body had been immaculately blacked-up, her head was still white and shiny where her wig had been. Feeling as though I was being rude staring, I tore my eyes away. Shuffling to my feet I stretched and padded through to the kitchen yawning and put the kettle on. As I was getting the milk out of the fridge I saw that once again my fridge magnets had been altered. To my disgust they now read 'hairy balls'. After a bit of thought as I waited for the kettle to boil I altered it to 'fairy falls'.

"Morning." Steph said yawning as she came into the kitchen as I was altering the rude magnets.

"Morning." I replied. "What is it with men and stupid childish rude words?"

"Oh that was mine." She said with a smile. "I got up in the night for a drink of water and spotted the 'tit' on there. I was trying to spell 'testicles' but I was too drunk."

"Oh." I drifted off into my thoughts for a minute. "Is Carly up yet?"

"She's just taping her wig back on then she'll be in. She said she'll have a coffee if you're making one. Mine's a tea please?"

**

Once Carly and Stephanie had gone I collapsed to die happily in peace after god knew how many junior paracetamol. I was starting to feel a little better and at least I wasn't being sick this time.

I was just starting to nod off again on the sofa as I heard the living room door burst open.

"Mum?"

"Hm?" I murmured sleepily.

"Why do you have a top on that says you have chlamydia?"

That made me sit up with a start. "Sorry, I forgot about that." I pulled at the bloody t-shirt with disgust. I'd have to go and get a shower and get changed. I yawned and looked about me. "You know Paul, all morning I've had this awful feeling that I've forgotten something." I scratched my head with frustration before wincing at the dried whipped cream that had matted in there.

"Like the Bah mitzvah?"

I leaped up with a start. "Shit, shit, shit!" How

the hell had that slipped my mind? I'd been frantic about the upcoming Bah mitzvah all week and now it was actually here I was completely unprepared!

"Paul, here, take my bank card and go draw fifty quid out of the cash machine down the road. I'll write my pin number down." I pulled my handbag out from underneath the sofa and held out my card to him.

He shook his head at me. "I can't, I'm late for football practice. What do you need fifty quid for anyway?"

"To stick in the card. Oh God where did I put the card?" I rummaged through my bag in a panic "Shit! Where's the bloody card?"

"You're giving them fifty quid? For someone you don't even know?"

"A Bah mitzvah's an important event."

"But you aren't Jewish!"

I pulled the card from the back of my bag with relief. "Today I am!"

***

After showering and getting changed I calculated I just had time to run up to the cash machine at the top of our road before the bus would arrive. I hurried up the road as fast as I could in the kitten heels that I had bought for the occasion. Out of breath and with a stitch I arrived at the cash machine. I took a moment to get my breath back as I pulled the card out of my purse and slid it into the slot in front of me. To my dismay, before I even had chance to enter my pin, a message popped up onto the screen.

YOUR CARD HAS BEEN SUSPENDED
DUE TO A SECURITY BREACH. PLEASE
CONTACT YOUR LOCAL BRANCH.

I stared at it in disbelief. "NO!" I was stunned. "You can't do this to me! Not today!"

Try as I might, the machine wasn't interested in hearing about my religious predicament. I slid down the wall and sat on the floor below the machine. Now what? I couldn't contact my local branch until Monday. Shit.

"What the hell can I do about a present for the Jewish boy?" I rummaged through my purse to see if I had any cash tucked away in there. All I could find was my bus fare ready in one compartment, and a few pennies and a random euro in the other. I snapped my purse shut with a sigh. I could feel tears starting to prick at the back of my eyes and a lump was forming in my throat.

"Are you okay there, Miss?" A voice asked from above.

I shook my head as I had no voice thanks to the lump in my throat.

"Are you hurt?" The voice asked.

I shook my head for a moment before changing my mind and nodding as tears burst down my cheeks. I looked up and saw the voice belonged to a traffic warden. Oh just bloody typical!

I sniffed the tears back as she sat down next to me. I eyed her nervously through my tears as she sat on the pavement beside me.

"Whatever's wrong?" She asked.

I tried speaking but found that I couldn't form words for the sobs. I tried gesturing with my hands my predicament whilst the only words that sounded legible were - "I can't afford a Bah mitz-vah."

To her credit, the traffic warden was very sweet as she walked me home and told me not to worry, and that I was probably too old for a Bah mitzvah anyway.

Once I had got rid of her -after assuring her several times that I did not live alone and I wasn't a danger to society- I set about rummaging through the house in a desperate attempt to find something that I could wrap-up as a gift. Unfortunately, Max had gone out so I couldn't ask him for money, and there wasn't a penny in the house. After desperately looking around for something that would be suitable for a thirteen-year-old boy, I finally settled on the large new atlas that I had bought Paul for the previous Christmas. He wouldn't mind, I could always buy him a replacement when my bank card was re-instated. In a mad rush I wrapped it up in the only gift wrap that I had and hoped it wouldn't be too inappropriate -it was Peppa Pig wrapping paper- I knew they didn't eat pigs so did that mean they worshipped them as Indians do with Cows? I cursed my ignorance and hoped for the best as I didn't have time to Google it.

With seconds to spare I made it to the bus stop as the bus was just arriving.

Chapter Eighteen

I was more than a little nervous as I approached the door to the bah mitzvah; I could hear music and merriment from outside. Taking a deep breath, I smoothed my hair back, fixed a grin to my face and opened the door.

Everyone looked to be having a wonderful time and I felt very much the intruder as I slid around the perimeter looking for somewhere to hide until I could spot Fiona, say hello, give her son the gift and then leave quickly and quietly without causing anyone offense.

I finally settled myself to the right of the small bar that had been set up across from the main doors. After being informed by the barman that it was a free bar, I accepted an orange juice and decided to try out the 'lingo' by thanking him with a 'mazal tov'. He looked at me strangely so perhaps I hadn't used my newly learned term correctly? I sat on the edge of a cast iron radiator in the dark corner and tried to make myself as inconspicuous as possible.

By the time I had got down the bottom of my glass I was spotted by Fiona, who came rushing over to welcome me.

"I'm so glad you came!" She gushed. "Is your family not with you?" She asked as she looked about me.

"Thank you for inviting me." I returned. "I'm sorry I'm the only one who could make it today. My husband and son were a bit tied up."

"Don't worry about it. I know it was a bit short notice. Like I said, I had no idea you were Jewish. I've never seen you at any of our celebrations. Are you new to the area?"

"No, we've been here for quite a while. Just not really...not...giving religion as much time as maybe we should?"

"Oh I hear you." She laughed softly. "In this day and age who has time for anything? We're all run off our feet just trying to make ends meet aren't we?"

"Yes." I said with relief. "I've been trying to run a household, hold down a full time job, and trying to keep everybody happy. To be honest, I'm exhausted with it all."

"I know exactly what you mean. They never appreciate all that we do for them do they."

We lapsed into a slightly awkward silence as we stood together watching her son having fun with some other young boys across the room. He caught her eye and waved over at us.

"Samuel! Come over here a minute!" She called.

He nodded and came over towards us, narrowly

avoiding being mowed down by two pensioners that were dancing with abandon.

"Come and meet Claire. She lives down the road from us."

"Hi." He said shyly offering me his hand.

"Nice to meet you Samuel." I replied shaking his hand. "Thank you for inviting me."

Remembering the gift I still had tucked under my arm, I fumbled it into his hands. "This is for you." I smiled nervously. "Sorry about the wrapping paper."

"Thank you very much." He looked unsure at Peppa pig as he pulled away the paper.

Fiona nodded her approval to me at the atlas I had given her son. I was very relieved that I had made the right choice of last minute gift after all.

All was going splendidly until Samuel opened the atlas, revealing a segment that had been cut-away from inside the book to create a secret compartment -that contained to my horror - a roll of cherry flavoured condoms.

I felt my stomach drop as Samuel slid on a pair of glasses that he pulled from out of his pocket, and held up the roll of foil packets to read what it said on the packet. He dropped them with a start as his eyes focused on the word 'CONDOM'.

A hush seemed to fall over the room as all eyes appeared to turn to me in disgust.

I backed up against the wall intending to slide my way slowly towards the exit. No-one said a word to me, they didn't have to, their shock and fury was obvious. I froze as a whisper seemed to dance about the building as people stared at me. *Pervert...* **Pervert...PERVERT!**

"They're not mine." I whispered around me. "I don't even like cherry flavour!"

As my paralysis broke, I ran from the room as fast as my legs would carry me. I ran all the way to the bus stop at a speed that would have beaten Forrest Gump and sobbed until the bus arrived and let me aboard.

***

"Coo-ee!" My new friend Violet called from across the almost empty bus." She patted the seat next to her. "How are you?"

I sat down sadly in the seat next to her with a bump.

"Oh, as bad as that?" She commented after taking in my mascara covered cheeks.

I nodded.

She looked to be racking her brain trying to think of something to say to me. Finally, she settled on– "I like your dress."

"Thanks."

She looked about her, desperate for something to say to break the awkward silence. "Oh, I've just remembered, last time I saw you you'd just bought a Jewish menorah to deter the Jehovah's Witnesses.

How did that turn out?"

I put my head in my hands and cried.

"Oh dear, oh dear!" She tutted.

I got my sobs under control and looked up at her earnestly. "I'm Jewish now you know!"

She did a double take. "I beg your pardon?" She paused. "I don't think owning a menorah automatically makes you Jewish, honey."

I nodded. "It's true, I've just been to a bah mitzvah and everything."

"Oh." She looked taken aback. "Well, as religions go I suppose they are one of the nicer ones."

"I just gave a young Jewish boy some cherry flavoured condoms."

"Oh…." She flushed. "Did he…like them?"

"Not by the look on his face."

She looked off to one side with raised eyebrows.

"I didn't mean to give him condoms, I meant to give him an atlas."

"That's quite a mistake!"

"I know!"

***

As I arrived home I slid my front door key into the lock and noticed straight away the pair of expensive Italian stilettos kicked off carelessly at the bottom of my stairs. From high above me I heard a throaty giggle coming from my bedroom. I froze to the spot. *They* were HERE! They were doing *it*, HERE! Max and Lola, **IN MY BED**! I felt my stomach muscles tighten and my jaw clench as a quiet rage eclipsed my brain, pouring a wave of adrenalin through the very fibre of my being. I think I felt a kind of 'pop' as a sense of calm yet nervous energy enveloped me as I marched up the stairs to confront my destiny.

Chapter Nineteen

I leaped up the steps two at a time before stopping outside my bedroom door. Pausing for a moment, I could hear the moaning and groaning going on through the door. I stood there for a couple of seconds more before fixing my face into a blank expression and flung the door open.

At once I was confronted by the sight of Lola riding my husband in -what *Jackie Magazine* used to refer to as - the reverse cowgirl.

"What the hell?" Screamed Lola as she tried desperately to cover her breasts with her hands. (Reassuringly saggy, I thought.) She wiggled away across the bed from Max as he laid there looking what I can only describe as shocked and 'wilting'. I, meanwhile had decided to ignore the pair of them and go about my usual business. After all, it was my bedroom too, and I would be damned if I allowed myself to be driven out by 'The Tart'! I looked around at my messy bedroom in dismay. No, this wouldn't do. This wouldn't do at all.

"What the hell are you doing?" Max exclaimed as I picked his trousers up off the floor and calmly hung them on a coat hanger. I then made a show of shaking all of the creases out of his shirt and sliding that onto a coat hanger too before hanging them up carefully in the wardrobe. Next I turned my attention to his underpants.

"There's skid marks in these." I observed before turning the gusset outwards and showing Lola. "What do you think will get that stain out?"

She had her hands over her mouth in shock and kept looking to Max to explain this strange new set of circumstances.

"She's gone mad!" He said incredulously. "She's finally lost the bloody plot!"

"Pardon?" I enquired, as I had been busy folding Lola's skirt and hadn't really being paying that much attention. I picked her bra up off the floor next and sniffed it. "Phew that's a bit whiffy isn't it." I dropped it into the clothes-hamper next to the bed along with Max's underpants.

Satisfied that the bedroom floor was now tidy, I turned my attention to the bed. I like my bed to be tidy and this ruffled mess wouldn't do at all. Smoothing out the duvet cover turned out to be a bit problematic as Lola was desperately trying to pull the covers further up to her chin -which was annoying me greatly as I was trying to do a nice neat job of making the bed.

"Do something Max!" She whined.

I stood back to observe my handiwork with my hands on my hips, nodding in satisfaction. I had now picked up and folded all of the clothes from the floor, and made the bed. Yes, the bedroom was looking much better, much more normal. Just having it tidy was making me feel better already. I thought for a moment, now what was next in my normal bedroom routine? Oh yes that was it. I picked up my hairbrush from the bedside table and began to brush Lola's hair.

"MAX!" She screamed, as she tried to throw me off.

"Keep still!" I ordered as I grabbed her head with one hand and tried to aim my hairbrush with the other.

Max leaped out of bed with a start, looking about him for something to hide his shrivelling manhood behind. After finding nothing to cover himself with, he gave up and tried to restrain me as he *was - el -bollocko*.

"Get that thing away from me!" I roared at him as I hit his offending member with the back of my hairbrush. Once he was swiftly disabled and on the floor crying I resumed brushing Lola's hair.

"Oh, don't cry silly." I soothed. "If you just keep still till I've finished I won't have to pull at the knots so much."

Now what happened next is a little hazy. I *do* remember fragments of the rest of 'the incident' but some details do elude me. Such as how I got Lola into the bath, I don't know. I just remember this feeling of her being very dirty and needing a good wash. I seem to remember that Alan Partridge was in the bathroom with me, sitting on the toilet; he seemed to think it was a good idea to 'relax in the bath'. As I held Lola's head under the cold tap I remember instructing her. "Listen to Alan Partridge, he knows what he's on about!"

"What?" she cried as I banged her head on the tap.

"Just RELAX!" I ordered, as I poured cold water over her head and scrubbed her forehead with the loofa.

The next thing that I recall is Max charging me from behind and knocking me over. I think I must have hit my head on the way down or something as I think I blacked out for a few seconds. I came round confused and with a thumping headache to find that I was bound at the wrists and tied to the radiator with what looked like my pink dressing-gown belt. I remember feeling like Terry Waite as I sat there slightly startled, tied to my bathroom radiator, whilst my husband's tart sat shivering on the toilet lid glaring at me.

I peered behind her, "Where's Alan Partridge gone?"

Chapter Twenty

The therapist stared at me in silence for what seemed like an eternity. I didn't care for the intensity of her gaze or the fact that she suddenly seemed incapable of blinking. Feeling uncomfortable, I looked away and concentrated on the sign on the wall that stated – *Violent or Threatening Behaviour Towards Our Staff Will Not Be Tolerated.* I briefly wondered if mocking their religion in song counted?

"So…" She announced, breaking the silence. "Now we're getting to the crux of your reason for being here."

"Yes?"

"To sum it up, it appears to me that you had a brief mental breakdown after suffering from marital problems and employment problems; coupled with your deep routed fear that you may be a racist, everything culminated into this…episode. The things you *did* may make no sense to you, but in a strange kind of way they make perfect sense to me. Think about it, you believed your bedroom was dirty and soiled from your husband's affair, so you tidied it; you believed your husband's mistress was dirty and so you forced her to have a wash; in a strange kind of way your sub-conscious was trying to deal with your problems, it just lost sight of the boundaries a little." She paused for a moment. "What I don't comprehend though, is why you insisted Alan Partridge was sitting on your toilet?"

"He was definitely there, he was sitting on the toilet and telling Lola to relax."

"But why Alan Partridge?"

"Well, the only reason I can think of is from the relaxation cd I was listening to in the bath; I thought the man on the tape sounded like Alan Partridge, and he kept telling me to relax."

She flicked back through her notes carefully. "Ah yes, you did mention Alan Partridge, the night before the Bah mitzvah I believe."

"My blood runs cold just at the thought of the dreaded 'B-word' as I now think of it. The B-word where I gave the J-boy the C-words!"

"You do that a lot, I've noticed."

"I do what?"

"Abbreviate. Why do you do that?"

"I don't know." I shrugged.

"Never mind. Okay I can see how Alan Partridge could have been in your mind now. We'll just put that to one side for now. Am I right in assuming that you don't actually care that your husband was having an affair, but what really galled you was him having an affair in your marital bed?"

"He could've been more discrete." I sulked.

"Have you thought that you should perhaps go for marriage guidance counselling? Or maybe even, given your recent circumstances, getting a divorce?"

"We're going to wait for TLS to get through his education first, then we'll get a divorce."

"But what about you and your happiness? Doesn't your happiness matter just as much as your husband and son's?"

I sniffed. "I get by."

She burst out with a snort that I didn't feel was very professional. "No you don't!"
She pulled her chair a little closer to me and spoke a little softer. "You aren't 'getting by', not by any stretch of the imagination. People that are 'getting by' generally don't get sectioned under the mental health act."

I felt a little tear starting in the corner of my eye. I blinked it away quickly. YOU WILL NOT CRY! I ordered my eyeballs.

"Why do you think you are in this position now Claire? What do you think is the single thing that led you to be here in this place? What was the very first cause of all your problems? Cast your mind back to the very beginning."

"The pube."

"The pube? The pube in the jam tart? You believe that one single event is what led you to be in this position?"

I nodded. It was obvious wasn't it? "If it

wasn't for that pube I wouldn't have got the sack and become unemployable; I wouldn't have been home to answer the door to the salesman whom I assaulted with a school shoe; I wouldn't have been home to answer the door to all the religious nutters that have driven me round the twist; Bobert wouldn't know all about my menstrual cycle, *and* I wouldn't have rung up that poor telesales girl and asked what colour her knickers were." I paused for breath. "And…because I wouldn't have been home to answer the door to the god squad, they wouldn't have driven me into buying the menorah, so I wouldn't have had the humiliation with the bar mitzvah; I wouldn't have discovered my son's condoms in his atlas so I wouldn't have his sex life to worry about, *and*… if I hadn't gone to the bah mitzvah, Max wouldn't have brought home the tart for me to wash!" I think I made my point!

The therapist was staring at me again.

"I'm sorry," I continued, "but I'm right. It's the pube!"

She shook her head in annoyance. "I also don't think it's any coincidence that you call your husband's mistress a…" She looked down at her notes. "…a dirty tart. Not unlike your dirty jam tart?"

I shrugged. I didn't really see the connection.

She paused for a while, giving me an assessing look. "What is the relevance of the homeless woman you insist on feeding?"

Shit. She caught me off-guard with that one. I

wasn't expecting her to pick up on that. She was staring at me waiting for me to answer.

"Well? Why do you worry for her so much? As you said in your story, you told her about the homeless shelter she could go to for help. Why do you feel you have to be the one to help her?"

I scowled. She'd found my Achilles heel. I shrugged indifferently.

She was watching me closely as she pulled another folder from out of her immense holdall. I sat a little stiffer as I suspected what it might be.

"This is a police report from two years ago." She paused heavily. "There was an accident in the town centre where a homeless person was accidently run down by a motorist. Do you want to tell me about it?"

I looked away.

"I've read the report Claire. It is quite obvious that it was an accident. In no shape or form was it your fault. You were never thought to be at fault. Several witnesses came forward that exonerated you." She paused. "Is that why you don't drive anymore?"

I nodded and looked away.

"And is that why you felt Max wouldn't approve of you looking after the homeless woman? Did you think he'd see it as a sign of guilt or weakness?"

I nodded. I didn't trust my voice.

"So, do you still think it's the pube that was the single event that caused this breakdown?"

I shook my head as a tear started to roll down my cheek.

Chapter Twenty-One

I was sitting in a little waiting room waiting for Max to come and fetch me home. I felt as if I'd been through the ringer after the last session of therapy and for once I was actually looking forward to seeing Max. I was allowed to go home now as they didn't believe I was a danger to society and thankfully 'The Tart' wasn't going to press charges. I was just under instruction to keep seeing the therapist once a week until I was deemed 'back to normal!'

"Hey." Max said softly as he peered around the door. "Are you ready?"

"Ready as I'll ever be."

***

The house seemed so alien to me now; I had been gone three days yet it felt like a lifetime had passed since I was last there. Things had changed. I think I had changed. I looked around the cold unfriendly living room with indifference.

"You hate me don't you." He said softly as he dropped the car keys onto the sideboard.

"I really don't." I shook my head. "I should, but I don't. Our marriage has been over for a long time hasn't it?"

He nodded. "It's not been the same since the accident with that bloody homeless girl. You just seem to...shrivel away, bit by bit."

"I did. And I'm sorry for that. I just couldn't cope with ending someone's life like that. I couldn't be close with you anymore; I didn't feel like I deserved affection... so I pushed you away. I see that now."

"It wasn't your fault that girl jumped out in front of your car. There was no way on earth you could have stopped in time. There was nothing you could've done different."

I sat down next to him on the sofa. "I know, really I do. It's just that I can't forget it. Something in me died the day that girl went under my wheels. You don't know what it was like."

"You've never spoken about it before." He observed quietly.

"I've never been able to before. I've spent the last two years trying scrub it from my brain."

"Perhaps it's a good thing that things have come to a head at last."

"Maybe." I sighed sadly. "I just wish I could have had a breakthrough without giving a young boy cherry-flavoured condoms for his birthday and having Alan Partridge tell me to half-drown a tart."

That caught his attention sharply. "What now? Cherry flavoured condoms?"

"Oh, I forgot to tell you about that bit." I waved my hand distastefully. "Suffice to say the Bah mitzvah didn't go well."

He looked away baffled.

I sank morosely into my own thoughts.

"I didn't really want Lola you know." He said resting his hand on mine. "It was a stupid cry for attention. I was lonely. I missed you."

"I know. I'm sorry."

"The more you ignored what was going on, the more hurt I felt. I wanted you to feel jealous, to make you fight for me *and* to hurt you like I was hurting. It's selfish, I know, and I'm sorry."

"I know."

"Don't leave me!"

"We both know this is going nowhere. But, I'll stay, for now."

"Lola's gone. Just so you know. It's over."

"Good, because God – and Alan Partridge - only knows what I'd do to her next time."

Chapter Twenty-Two

"Everything's okay." I told the therapist three months later when she asked how things were going. I hadn't seen her for a few months as she'd been off work with 'stress,' or so I'd been told by her replacement - who was now also off with 'stress.'

"Now when you say okay does that mean things are going better, or is it that you want me to stop asking questions?"

Bloody hell this woman really had me sussed out! I waved my hand back and forwards. "Things are better than they were."

"In what way better?" She had a pen hovering over a bit of paper that could well be a Sudoku puzzle for all I knew.

"Well the tart's gone for a start."

"The jam tart or the tart-tart? Gosh I hate that word." She shuddered.

"Both!" I laughed.

"Good, good. So any more outbursts of temper?"

"Outbursts? Oh, mm."

"What does that mean?" She started clicking her pen with annoyance.

"Do you want me to try and explain?" I looked up at the clock. "It might take a little while."

"Be my guest!" She said with a sarcastic flourish of her arms.

I eyed her a little confused. "Okay then."

***

"Okay. Well, when I got home from the hospital, Max and me had a really good heart-to-heart. We stayed up all night talking about...everything really. I opened up a bit about how traumatised I was from the car accident where the homeless girl died. Max was really supportive about it. I always thought that deep down he must have thought that it was my fault. Back when I was a driver he used to criticize my driving all the time and tell me how I'd almost killed this person on a bike or that pedestrian over there that was hopping was my fault as I'd run over his foot on a zebra crossing. Let me see, oh yes, another one of his favourites was - wing mirrors aren't for decoration...There's other gears besides third...Reverse parking isn't guesswork.... You get the gist. So I thought there's no way on earth he'd believe me when I said it wasn't my fault, so I clammed up about it. Bottled it up, I think. Anyway, we had a long talk about it all and he's on my side; says he doesn't blame me at all. I feel like a great burden's been lifted.

We spent the rest of the night talking about 'The Tart' and how it all started. He said it's all over now. And you know what, call me a naive idiot, but I believe him. In fact, after a few days of *really* talking properly to each other I gave in to Max and told him that I'd give marriage guidance a try. I knew we'd probably be splitting up eventually anyway, so what did I really have to lose by going?

***

"I feel like a naughty little school boy." Max whispered as the marriage guidance councillor (*Call me Barry!*) left us alone for a moment while he went to fetch a box of tissues.

I whispered back, "I think it's a little unprofessional for a therapist to cry, don't you?"

"He's a bit sensitive isn't he!"

"Sorry about that!" Barry exclaimed as he burst back into the room armed with man-size Kleenex. "Occupational hazard I'm afraid." He dabbed at his eyes dramatically.

Max and I shared a 'look'. Trust us to get Mr Newage Sensitive!

"So, as you previously disclosed, things started to sour between you both after the unfortunate car accident. Affection got lost along the wayside, along with your sex life -which culminated in the affair with the...erm...tart, as you put it." He looked at me disapprovingly as he said the T word.

I'm sorry, I know it's not very PC but it's the only word that comes to mind when I think of her. I obviously spent too many hours watching Ma Boswell chasing *Lilo Lil* down the street and calling her a tart on the sit-com *Bread*.

"Okay, we've spent the last hour discussing how things have gone wrong in your marriage. No marriage is perfect, and things do go wrong. Especially in the bedroom, and if it's not right in the bedroom then generally it's not right anywhere else either. *So* I think that's the best place to start." He clapped his hands together enthusiastically. "So let's start trying to fix things eh?"

"What do you suggest?" Asked Max.

"How comfortable are you with role play?"

Oh shit. What the hell was he on about? I agreed to marriage guidance counselling, not sex therapy! I could feel my cheeks starting to colour up already.

"What do you have in mind?" Max asked.

I was freaking out quietly behind a fixed grin. *Oh please let this not be a sex thing! Dear God, if this is a sex thing, and if you do exist, this would be the perfect moment to prove your existence by opening up the ground beneath me and allowing me to escape with my dignity* intact!

"What I have in mind..." Barry continued, oblivious to my discomfort, "is for you to freshen things up a bit."

"Go on?" Max said to him, leaning forward with a little more enthusiasm than I expected.

"What I want you both to do...get dressed up;

go out – separately – and meet up somewhere. Pretend it's the first time you've met. Make up new names, histories and character traits. Really go back to basics."

WHAT? What the hell was this nutter on about?

"You think it'll help?" Max asked.

"I really do. You need to reconnect with each other, really get to know each other again. But, for the night, be different people. Be the people you would want to be. Fantasise a little. Make it fresh, new, exciting. Why not meet up in a hotel bar? Maybe book a room in case things go well."

WHAT?

"Claire." He said making me jump. "Who do you want Max to be? Who do you fantasize about?"

Oh God! Please leave me alone, please leave me alone, please leave me alone.

"Come now," he said, "there must be someone you fantasize about Claire? Some fantasy scenario that you think about?"

"No thank you." I said and crossed my ankles firmly.

"Are you not comfortable talking about sex?"

I could feel my face going scarlet and my palms getting sweaty. "That's...that's private thank you very much."

He considered me thoughtfully for a moment. "What do you think about using sex aids?"

Oh my god I'm going to faint!

"They can be very useful spicing up a marriage that's gone a bit stale. Just something to consider?"

Please stop staring at me!

"So what do you think Claire?"

What did I think? WHAT DID I THINK? I think I wanted to grab the bastard by his rainbow coloured braces and twang them till his nipples bled! If he mentioned my unmentionables, I'd be kicking him in his unmentionables! I rushed to my feet and grabbed my handbag before my temper could escape me. "I think it's getting very late. Look at the time Max, we best get going if we're going to beat rush hour."

Chapter Twenty-Three

I had never been so embarrassed in my entire life. No scrap that, that's not entirely true, but this was the most embarrassed I'd been for a while, since I gave the J-boy the C-words at the B-word anyway.

I was sitting in the passenger seat of Max's red penis extension - lost in thought when I felt Max's hand rest on my knee. I stared at the offending thing for a moment before remembering that I'm supposed to be trying to feel affection for his appendages. Instead of slapping it away as I felt like doing, I rested my own hand on the top of it softly. Fake it 'till you make it, right?

"Well that was an experience." He said.

"You said it."

He glanced over at me for a moment. "So what did you think?"

What did I think? I thought he was nuts! But I compromised on - "I don't know; I was a bit overwhelmed." (Understatement.) "What did you think?"

"I think he might have a point."

WHAT?

He continued. "I quite like the idea of us meeting up somewhere, *incognito.* I think it sounds like fun. A good way to let our hair down and reconnect without all the bad stuff creeping into the conversation. You know, just starting on a fresh page."

I must reiterate – *WHAT*?

I stared down at the hand on my knee and gave an involuntary shudder. What would this endeavour entail? Do people do this all the time? Is this normal? Oh God please don't let it be dressing up in a blonde wig and donning crotchless knickers!

I couldn't find the words to reply, so I responded with a squeeze of his hand. When I got home I would google it.

***

Okay, I googled it. Apparently it is a *thing* that some people do to spice up their marriages. Well, that's all well and good for them, but I'm not that sure that I even *want* my marriage, spicy or otherwise. Somehow I seemed to have been railroaded into the farcical scenario and yes, I know it *is* my own fault really, I know. I should have stood up to the so-called marriage guidance counsellor and told him to stick his crotchless knickers and sex aids where the sun don't shine. But it was difficult to say no to Max. Despite all his faults -and there are more than a few- he does actually appear to love me. Who knew! I know he really wants things to work out now everything's out in the open, I'm just not sure that I do. But where would I go? I have no job, no money. There's no way I could take Paul with me. I'd end up back living with my mother! I think I need time to make up my mind. It was a conundrum. I rattled the choices around my brain. Do I stay and play dress up with Max, or do I leave and go live with my mother?

***

"Hold still Hun," said Carly as she started gluing the – what I can only describe as - *Dolly Parton* hairpiece to my head.

"It's itchy." I complained.

She gave me a stern look before pulling off her own wig and pointing out how sore her own scalp was. "At least you have hair as a buffer. Stop whinging and deal with it."

"Okay." I sulked.

She took a moment to adjust her hair in the mirror before returning her attention to me. "I think you're crazy you know?"

I grimaced a little. "I know. I just can't go live with my mother. Given the choice between crotchless knickers and my mother there's no contest."

She paused and stared in disbelief at me for a moment in the mirror -tail comb in hand. "Life isn't that black and white. Surely you have more choices than that? It can't be just crotchless knickers or you mother? Has Max even *mentioned* crotchless knickers?"

"No but I read it on the internet."

"It's not like *Simon says!*"

"I don't mean I'm *actually* going to wear crotch-less knickers, it's just the words *crotchless knickers* seem to sum up this whole stupid idea."

"I don't know why you're going along with it. You don't even like Max."

I shook my heavy head at her. "My therapist said I'm supposed to be tackling life head-on now, to stop being a victim and start taking control. Well this is taking control isn't it. I'm taking control and deciding not to go live with my mother."

"What does your son make of all this?"

I arched my eyebrows as I pondered. "Hard to tell. He seems pretty indifferent about mine and Max's relationship. We've both spoken to him about the possibility of us splitting up; the only thing he was really interested in - was if that meant he'd get twice as much for Christmas!"

She shook her head at me. "Kid's eh?"

"You said it!"

"I still think you're crazy though, going along with this charade. Just pack him in and be done with it. So what if you have to stay with your mother for a little while until you get back on your feet."

She might not get it, but I know what I'm doing. "Look, one night of dress-up while I make my mind up what I want from life, is much better than the testicle shrivelling experience of staying with my mother."

"Oh yeah? What do you know about shrivelling

testicles?"

Oh shit. I forgot who I was talking to. Had I put my foot in it? I felt my face colour up a little. "I'm not implying that I know what it's like to have shrivelling testicles, I'm just going off what Max describes after being in her presence for a while."

She carried on fiddling with my hair. "Well I can tell you all about shrivelling testicles if you want? But it doesn't make for polite conversation."

I looked at her out of the corner of my eye. Had I offended her?

"Sorry." I offered. "I forgot."

"It's okay. It isn't for much longer and they'll be a bad dream."

"Well if you don't want to wait that long, come to my mum's for tea, she'll probably hand them to you in a bag by the time you leave."

I gasped in horror as the words had slipped un-edited from my mouth. I looked to Carly for her re-action, who was thankfully laughing. Phew!

"I'm terrified to be honest with you." She admitted after a while. "I've been begging for this operation for years, and now that it's nearly here... well...I feel sick. On the one hand, I can't wait to get it over with and get on with my life, but on the other hand, there's a small part of me that finds it so...scary. There's so many things that can go wrong. Once it's done there's no going back is there."

"I'm afraid not. You aren't getting cold feet are

you?"

"It's complicated. I just don't – and never have felt male. I feel like a girl. I couldn't go back to trying to live like a man again. I just sometimes wonder...occasionally...if I should maybe stay as I am, my own fabulous self," she said with a laugh, "just with one little flaw. Well between you and me, not so little."

I didn't know what to say. I'd never had a transgender friend before. This was all a little new to me. I shook my head at her dilemma. "I thought I had a hard choice between crotchless knickers or my mother. Your choice is penis or no penis."

She nodded sagely. "That is the question."

***

After an hour of being poked and prodded at, Carly decided that I was 'ready'.

"Ta-da!" She announced as she spun me around to face the mirror.

I gazed in horror at the sight that met my eyes. My new hair was piled up on top of my head a good twelve inches above my forehead making me look like the love child of Dolly Parton and Donald Trump.

"Lovely!" I told Carly with a polite grimace. The twitch was definitely back in my left eye. "And how long will this last for?"

"Oh it'll last ages. The hair pieces are glued in, so they should stay in for about a fortnight if you're careful."

PARDON? A FORTNIGHT? My stomach sank down through my knees. "That's brilliant." I gulped. "Thank you." I added.

"No problem at all Hun, I love messing about with hair."

Can't disagree with the messing about part.

"It really suits you." She carried on fiddling with the offending crow's nest affectionately. "So what are you wearing?"

Oh God no! I thought.

"I've got just the thing." She grinned.

Chapter Twenty-Four

I looked at my watch nervously as I left Carly's flat. I had about half-an-hour to kill before I had to meet Max -or whatever he would be calling himself – at the hotel across the street. I had made my excuses to Carly in an effort to escape her clutches before she could make me look any more ridiculous than I already felt.

I caught sight of my reflection in a shop window as I hurried past a woman who was trying to accost me with a clipboard.

"Excuse me…" She called after me.

I was too busy staring at the Dolly Parton in drag look-a-like I could see over her shoulder reflecting back at me.

"Hello? Do you have a moment?" She barged up

into my face making me jump.

"I have several," I told her, "but they're not for you."

She stared after me as I set off at a run - to head for the nearest shop in which to buy a coat to cover up the hideous outfit I was wearing. I looked across as I ran and noted Dolly Parton running alongside me from the mirrored façade of the building. We scowled at each other as we ran, taking in each other's sequined boob tube full of chicken fillets. For a brief moment I wondered at the irony of chickens being used as stuffing and not just the victims of it.

I lost Dolly as I ran up the steps and into Marks & Sparks, pausing briefly to stare at the sign for some indication where the coat and handbag department might be. Once satisfied that I knew where I was going, I headed off to buy a mac.

I left the department store a lot calmer than I arrived. I told the sales girl that my mac didn't need wrapping, I would be wearing it.

"Good idea." She said curtly. "I mean, it's going to rain isn't it." She corrected herself.

I knew exactly what she meant.

I made it back down the road to the posh hotel where I had arranged to meet Max just in the nick of time. I entered the grand lobby nervously. Looking about me I noticed the bar was located to the left of a large mirror. With trepidation I took a moment to view myself properly in the large ornate mirror before I went into the bar. Good God! I looked terrible. I looked like I should be auditioning for *Pricilla Queen of the Desert.* I self-consciously pulled at my beehive of a head in despair. Oh well, it was too late now, best to just get this charade over with.

I went to pull the large brass handle of the bar door when a hand suddenly blocked the way.

"Excuse me madam?"

I turned to face a young man in a grey designer suit who smelt of *KFC.* "Yes?" I asked him, feeling suddenly hungry.

"I can't let you go in there."

"Why what's wrong?"

He put a hand on my elbow and tried to pull me away from the entrance.

"Hey!" I cried.

"We don't want your sort in here. We're not that kind of hotel."

"I beg your pardon?" I pulled at the hand gripping my arm.

"Come on, if you leave quietly I won't call the police."

"The police? What for? What have I done?" I tried prying his fingers from off my wrist. "You're hurting me!"

"We don't' have..." he dropped his voice to a whisper. "We don't have *call-girls* in this hotel."

"WHAT? CALL-GIRL? ARE YOU INSANE?" I saw several guests turn to stare at me. "I'm here to meet my husband. I AM NOT A PROSTITUTE!"

He screwed his face up at me. "Oh yeah? And what's his name?"

"Max."

"Max yeah?"

"What, are you deaf? My husband Max is in *there!*"

He stood staring at me and shaking his head. Finally, he turned to his colleague across the lobby. "Stevo!" He yelled.

"What's up?" Stevo asked as he sauntered up.

"This *lady* here reckons her husband's in the bar waiting for her. They call him Max apparently. Just go and see if there's a Max in there will you."

I piped up. "He might not be calling himself Max tonight."

KFC breath then pulled me away from the door roughly. "Oh, you know what, I've had enough of this." He gripped my arm even tighter. "Stevo, get her other arm."

Between the two of them I was marched down the stone steps and cast out into the street head first where I collided with a Great-Dane that was in the middle of taking a shit. I don't know who was more surprised....me, the Great-Dane, or its owner who was hovering over his dog with a poop-a-scooper when Dolly Parton landed on him.

After disentangling myself carefully so as not to get dog shit on myself, I turned back to give the two 'suits' a piece of my mind. Sadly, they had dumped me out into the street and headed straight back inside. As I was peering through the door in search of them, it suddenly opened as a stern looking security guard came outside.

"Move along now love, there's a good girl." He said, whilst openly staring at my legs sticking out from beneath my mac.

"I could have them for assault!" I yelled over my shoulder as I retreated back down the steps.

Just TYPICAL! So now what? Max was inside that hotel right now waiting desperately for me to come in so he could chat me up. I sat down on the little wall of a fountain a few yards down from the hotel to think about things.

I could just not turn up, *but* how would that play out? Mm, he'd be hurt. He'd probably think I've stood him up and that I really do want a divorce. That would result in a row when we got home, and me being thrown out and banished to my mother's. Oh God no, I shook my head, I am NOT going to my mother's! So what was the alternative then? Getting past that bloody security guard and two suits. I got to my feet decisively; what was needed here was a disguise.

I headed back down the street towards Marks & Sparks. I didn't know what my disguise would be, but I hoped I'd get inspired by something once I was inside.

I ran once more up the front stairs to find to my dismay that it had shut. Bollocks! Now what?

I looked up and down the high street hoping

desperately for some shop to still be open. With a sigh of relief, I finally spotted a glow in a shop window off in the distance. Once more I set off at a sprint.

My relief was short lived as I got to the only store still open on the road - to find that it was a soft furnishings shop. I peered in through the window as I felt the rain start dripping down through the blonde wedding cake on my head. As a rain drop dripped down my nose I decided to go browse for a while in the shop while the rain stopped. If nothing else, it would give me somewhere dry to shelter while I re-grouped and thought of another plan.

I think the lightbulb went off above my head as I ambled down the bedding aisles. Inspiration took me as I spotted a king-size black bed sheet on special offer. I picked it for a moment in excitement before changing my mind and putting it back. No, I couldn't do *that*...could I?

After looking around the rest of the shop in vain, I had to bite the bullet and buy the bed sheet – along with a pair of haberdashery scissors.

Around the corner from the hotel, I ducked under an awning for shelter before pulling the black sheet out of the packaging. Could I really pull this off? I wondered as I cut out a letter box size hole in it to see out of. Oh well, what could it hurt?

Chapter Twenty-Five

The therapist interrupted me by raising her hand. "Please tell me you didn't."

"I did."

She put her hand across her mouth whilst staring at me in shock. "You can't *do* things like that! Don't you know what trouble and offense that could cause?"

"I do now."

She gestured for me to carry on whilst avoiding making eye contact.

***

"Okay, so I pulled the black sheet over my head and lined up the letterbox to see out of. I was surprised and pleased how well my disguise would work. I had hoped to buy an outfit to change from my hideous clothes but I hadn't given any thought to covering up my very obvious bee-hive of a head. This would work perfectly.

I dumped the bedding packaging in a litter bin as I made my way back around to the front of the hotel. I waltzed up the steps and past the security guard who looked towards me before pointedly looking away. Okay, at least I didn't have to worry about him recognising me, he obviously didn't feel comfortable making eye contact with me dressed as I was. Fine with me.

I approached the bar door once more, catching a slight glance of a Muslim woman with a tall head wearing a burka and six-inch red stilettos in the mirror as I passed. Without further impeachment I made it through the doors and into the bar. Success!

It took a moment for my eyes to adjust to the sombre lighting in the large half empty, art-deco space, but eventually I spotted the figure of Max seated up at the bar looking towards me.

As I walked towards him I had to admit he looked good. Gone was the typical sharp business suit he normally wore; now he was attired in jeans and a tight t-shirt showing off his muscular physique. For a moment I felt a little shy looking at him. He briefly cast his eye to my direction before returning his gaze to the doors behind me. As I approached him I noted how good he smelt. Some new cologne maybe?

I pulled up the stool next to him and perched on it. I remembered the rules. Tonight we did not know each other and so I didn't acknowledge him as I took a seat.

The bartender sauntered over my way eventually, giving me a distasteful look.

"Orange juice is it?" He remarked.

"Oh, no...vodka-martini please." And then as an afterthought I added, "Stirred, not shaken."

As I spoke, Max turned to me in surprise, obviously recognising my voice. He looked me up and down for what seemed like an eternity before looking away, shaking his head and downing his scotch.

I thought I better get this ball rolling before I lost the nerve.

"So.... you.... come here often?" I asked.

He turned to look at me with a strange expression that I couldn't quite fathom, before thoughtfully saying - "Yes. It's my hotel."

Crikey, he'd thought of a whole new identity!

"Well, it's very lovely."

"Thank you......?"

"Oh...Dolly. I'm Dolly."

"Nice to meet you Dolly, I'm Clint."

I nearly laughed but he looked so serious that I didn't dare.

He was looking me up and down puzzled. "What's with the outfit Dolly?"

I looked down self-consciously. "You'd probably prefer what I'm wearing underneath, but I was thrown out of the hotel for looking like a -" I dropped my voice. "-prostitute."

His eyes lit up a moment and a grin spread across his face as he shook his head.

"So I had to improvise to get past the security

guard."

"Very inventive *Dolly*."

"Thanks."

The bartender then brought me over the martini I had asked for.

"Let me get that for you Dolly." Max said paying the bartender for the drink. The poor bartender looked baffled at us but shrugged and pocketed the tip Max had given him.

I pulled the drink towards me before realising in alarm that I had no mouth to drink from. I had cut out the letterbox for my eyes but completely forgotten about a mouth hole.

"Could you please pass me that corkscrew?" I asked a passing waiter meekly.

"Of course madam." He said reaching over the bar and passing it to me.

"Thank you."

Once he was out of sight I used the corkscrew to make a little hole in my sheet for a mouth hole. Satisfied with my new aperture, I popped the corkscrew back onto the bar and wedged the straw of my drink through it.

"Mm." I said as the delicious cocktail slid down my throat before looking up in alarm as I heard Max -sorry Clint starting to choke.

"Are you okay?" I asked panicking as he started spluttering. After a moment I realised he had the giggles. Apparently my new straw hole was a step to far and now there he was in hysterics. The more I asked him – "What?" the worse he laughed.

"I'm sorry but I don't know what you find so funny Clint." I tutted.

He tried looking up at me but every time he did he burst out laughing again. I couldn't understand what was making him laugh so much? I reached up and pulled the straw from my face hole and sat back down in a huff to wait for his hysterics to stop.

While Clint was composing himself, I left to go use the ladies and to discard my bloody bed sheet - now that I was actually in the bar *and* with a husband who could verify that I *wasn't* a prostitute. I shrugged out of the bloody thing and hung it on the back of the toilet door before pulling the stupid chicken fillets from out of my boob-tube and discarding them into the bin.

I let myself out of the cubicle and approached the mirror to fix my face a little. Good God, Carly had definitely over-done it with the blusher, no wonder they thought I was a whore. Tutting, I blended as much of it away as I could before straightening my outfit. Next I began pulling at the bird's nest perched above my head with dismay. After furiously trying to flatten it a bit I was delighted to spot a basket of complimentary products that had been placed next to the sink for customers to use. I had a good rummage through the basket, before spotting a can of hairspray at the bottom. Just the thing! I pulled my hair down as flat as I could before giving it a really good blast.

I was quite taken aback when suddenly a smoke alarm went off above my head scaring the pants off me in the process. "Shit!" I exclaimed, whilst wafting the bloody thing to try and get it to shut up. This was just what I needed - attracting attention to myself when I was supposed to be barred.

I picked up a hand towel from the side of the sink and furiously wafted the offending thing for all I was worth. -Though I think I wafted a little too aggressively, as I managed to not only shut the thing up – but to knock it off the ceiling in the process. Bugger!

After trying several times to reach up and re-attach it to the ceiling, I finally gave up. I felt a slight wave of guilt as I carefully concealed the smoke alarm in the bin, hidden neatly beneath my discarded chicken fillets. Oh well, it was an innocent accident. Never mind.

With one last despairing look at my hair, I departed for the bar.

***

"Wow," said Max with a whistle as I sat down beside him.

I tossed my hair back smugly as I feigned indifference. It had to be an improvement on the bedsheet surely?

"So…Dolly. What do you….do for a living?"

198

I nearly said prostitute, god help me. I just suddenly had pretty woman in my head. I stopped myself just in time and for some strange reason said - "I'm a traffic warden." (I don't know where it came from.)

"Oh." He said. He fixed his face a moment as he began trying to get back on track again. "I...like a woman in uniform."

"You do – do you?" I racked my brain for something witty to return with. "How do you feel about.... clamps?"

"Nipple clamps?"

Oh, I was well out of my depth here. I picked up my drink and downed it quickly. "Another one of these please?" I called desperately to the bartender. I took a moment to panic before turning back to Max and whispering - "Not just nipples... testicles too?"

Okay perhaps that wasn't the right thing to say judging by the way he screwed his face up. Shit I really wasn't good at this. I downed the drink that was placed in front of me in one. The best thing I could do from here on in was to be quiet and only speak when spoken too. I nodded my head firmly before shaking my empty glass at the passing bartender.

I could hear the cogs ticking in Max's brain beside me as he tried to think of something to say. Eventually he settled on – "So how do you like your eggs in the morning?"

Oh come on. Even I could do better than that! I turned to him and shook my head. "We're really rubbish at this aren't we...Max."

He screwed his face up. "You know I thought we'd be good at this, but it's just stupid isn't it. How about we drop this stupid act, go order something to eat and then see about ordering a room? No funny business. Just a room...to sleep in. I don't want to put any pressure on you. The balls in your court in the bedroom."

I smiled. Despite the crappy chat up lines I was actually enjoying spending time with him. "Alright." I answered.

"Well alright then." He offered me his arm and led me over to a table in the corner. After pulling out my chair for me he handed me a menu and called for a waiter to take our drinks order. Now the charade of Dolly and Clint was over with, we actually had a really good time. We laughed like we hadn't in years, and when he put his hand on my knee I didn't get the urge to smack it like I normally would. In fact, by the time we'd finished dinner – and another four cocktails- I was nibbling his earlobe and pondering the idea of retiring to our room. I do believe that if we hadn't been interrupted as we had, then perhaps the evening would have ended much better than it did.

"What's that noise?" I asked Max, as he pulled me to my feet.

He stopped for a moment looking puzzled. "Fire

alarm?"

"Ambulance?" I wondered.

He both stared drunkenly towards the doors, swaying slightly as we held on to each other, when suddenly the doors burst open and armed police burst through the doors shouting "Freeze!"

Max and I continued swaying together as we tried to take in the whirlwind of activity that was going on around us.

"Is this part of the thing?" I slurred in Max's ear.

"What thing?"

"The thing – thing. Pretend identity thing." I looked about me worriedly.

***

After being rounded up like cattle, frisked and frog marched out of the building, we found ourselves being led back down the street towards Marks & Sparks where we ushered into the carpark and herded behind security fencing - by the bomb squad. Apparently a guest at the hotel had spotted - what they believed to be- a disused burka hanging on the back of a toilet door, and after closer inspection found what they thought to be semtex stuck to the top of the sanitary bin. They had then panicked and called the police.

After ascertaining that the so called 'semtex' was actually *my* discarded 'chicken fillets'- along with the remains of the smoke alarm, we were allowed to go back inside.

Chapter Twenty-Six

Although our 'date-night' had turned out to be a disaster, we still had fun and most definitely a night to remember. The following day Max observed that it would be a funny tale to tell the grandchildren one day. Mm, I thought. I still wasn't convinced about this staying together lark. True, the previous night had been fun – until the bomb squad thing, but...oh hell I didn't have a clue what I wanted anymore, to be perfectly honest. Max thought it would be a good idea for us to go on a few dates that coming week and try to connect again. I agreed as it might help me make my mind up a bit more about what I want. Plus, it was nice to get to know Max on friendly terms again. No longer was I thinking of him as a prat that I hated. True he had his faults, but so do I. I've been told a lot lately that it takes two to make a marriage fail and I think there might be something in that. Yes, we might still break up, but I think if that does happen, this time, we could stay friends.

I was twirling my wedding ring around my finger when I was disturbed from my thoughts by TLS brushing past me, wafting me with the pungent smell of Clearasil.

"Mum?"

"Hm?"

"You know I'm doing this history report on JFK?"

"The one you should have handed in last week you mean?"

He wrinkled his nose. "Yeah. Will you help me with it?"

"Let's have a look." I pulled the folder out of his hands and set it down on the breakfast table in front of me. "Let's see what you have so far then." I flipped open the cover to find that his three-thousand-word project -that should have been handed in a week ago, consisted of a single paragraph which probably contained around a hundred words.

"Paul!" I exclaimed, turning to bollock him. Lo and behold, he'd scarpered. "Just great! So this is *my* project now then is it?" I yelled.

"You said you was bored now you're not working!" The cheeky git called down the stairs.

"Yeah well…. you're adopted you know!"

"You wish!"

I huffed. Days like this I wish he was, just so that I could send him back!

I began to read his project: -

On the 22nd of November 1963, President Kennedy was travelling in an open top car in Dallas, when he was *shot three times. Witnesses said the shots came from the book suppository.*

Book *suppository?* Jesus Christ! What the hell did they teach kids in school these day? That books live up your bum? I read a little further on and it didn't get any better. Apparently Kennedy died from a *foetal* shot to the head!

I huffed to myself, this is gonna take all weekend.

***

The therapist interrupted me with a raise of her hand.

I was startled out of my story and fell silent.

"Okay," she said irately, "I don't know quite where to start!"

I shrugged.

"For starters, how can one person cause such chaos everywhere she goes?"

"Who?"

"Who? You!" She even pointed at me to really drive the point home.

"What are you talking about?" I was puzzled. "Do you mean the bomb squad thing? Because that really wasn't my fault. How was I to know that my chicken fillets would be mistaken for plastic explosives?"

She rested her head on her knees in despair giving me an unnecessary view of her dandruff falling down onto her red woolly tights. I thought she was behaving very unprofessionally, but I kept my thoughts to myself.

After a few moments she seemed to find her composure, straightened her glasses and sat back upright again. "Okay, let's put chicken-fillet-gate to one side." She paused. "Why do you feel the need to do your son's homework for him? Isn't it your job as a parent to ensure he does it himself?"

I felt a little ruffled. "He's fifteen. He's a moron. What he does now affects the rest of his life. By the time he's grown out of being a moron it'll be too late for him to retake his exams. If I can just get him into sixth form, hopefully the moron faze will pass and he'll knuckle down better."

"But what if he doesn't? Will you then take his A-levels for him so that he can go to university?"

"It won't come to that."

"It will if you continue letting him get away with passing all of his course work onto you!"

"I don't care for your tone!" I spluttered, feeling my temper starting to crack through.

"And I don't care - that you don't care for my tone!"

My right leg was starting to twitch uncontrollably. I took several deep breaths in an effort to calm down before I burst out with something rude or personal. The words that were trying to burst from my lips were – *And I don't care for your dandruff! Every time you shake your head at me I feel like*

I'm trapped in a snow-globe!

Several deep breaths later and I felt the rage pass a little. "I know what you're saying." I finally compromised. "Paul *should* do his own homework, frankly I'm sick of doing it! I just can't face the thought of him throwing his life away at such a young age. If he leaves school with no qualifications what would happen to him? What would he have to look forward to?" I sat further forward in my seat and pointed at the therapist. "I tell you what he'd have to look forward to - a rubbish job, a crappy house, a shitty life, until one day he finds a bloody pubic hair in his jam tart!"

"Oh not the bloody pube in the jam tart again!"

"I've told you before, everything comes back to that pube!" I nodded firmly.

"I'm sorry but you're just projecting your own problems onto your son."

I raised an eyebrow, "I love my son. I want what's best for him."

She continued staring at me for a moment before stopping to scribble something down on her pad. After she'd finished, she half-heartedly gestured me to continue where I had left off.

***

"Okay, the JFK project didn't take up too much of my time. There was so much information about it on the internet that it practically wrote itself- though the author of TLS's report should be credited as Wikipedia really. I just hoped I - I mean Paul - would get a good grade.

As for Max, he was being really sweet to me, I mean, REALLY sweet. It was like being wooed by a lover. He brought me flowers or chocolates every day on his way home from work, laughed at all my jokes – even though half the time I wasn't aware that I said anything funny, and best of all, he'd had 'the tart' transferred to a different building. He'd had to call it a promotion and bump her pay up so that she wouldn't be tempted to sue him, but from what he said, she seemed happy enough to move on. I think I'd scared her into keeping her distance from Max anyway.

This particular day, Max burst through the door armed with a bouquet of yellow roses in one hand and a bottle of wine in the other.

"Is that for me?" I asked with delight. I still wasn't at all used to being treated with such reverence.

"Oh yes." He said kissing me on the cheek. "And, how do you feel about coming away with me for a few days?"

"Away? Where?"

He put the wine and flowers down before fishing in his coat pocket for a moment. After rummaging around, he pulled out a set of keys and held them up excitedly. "How do you feel about boats?"

Chapter Twenty-Seven

It was very exciting when we walked up the riverbank to board the narrowboat that Max had hired for a few days. The sun was shining brightly high up above us, though we were spared the intensity of its heat by the soothing breeze that breathed its way over our skin.

As we made our way across the long grass, Max grabbed my hand to stop me sliding down the bank in my stupid boat shoes that were completely inadequate for navigating long grass. I quite liked the feeling of my hand in his and so left it there as we approached the pretty boat moored at the side of the river.

"Oh, it's beautiful." I observed as I stepped onto the painted boat, feeling its weight shift slightly underfoot.

"I knew you'd like it." Max grinned, stepping on behind me.

"I've always wanted to stay on a boat."

"I know."

I smiled and began to explore the little boat. Although it was very compact with being a narrowboat, it was very well appointed. It had a very long lounge area which included a little kitchen-ette, a little shower-room and toilet, followed on by a small bedroom at the end. Just the one bed-room I noted nervously. Oh well, I wouldn't worry about that for now, I'd hide under that bridge when I got to it. All in all, I was delighted with the little boat.

"When do we set sail?" I asked Max, clapping my hands together excitedly.

"We don't have sails you numpty," he chuckled, "but we'll set off anytime you like. I've already been instructed on how everything works. The locks should be fun."

"What do you mean?" I asked dimly. "You have the keys don't you?"

"The *water* locks. For when the water levels change."

"Oh, sorry."

We set sail, sorry, *set off,* not long after that. It was wonderful; Max was sat at the back of the boat steering whilst I sat beside him getting drunk in the sun on the bottle of rosé that he'd brought aboard. I've never really been much of a drinker up until the last few months but I was definitely start-ing to get a taste for it. Max turned to smile at me a little as I hiccupped.

"Sorry." I apologised before hiccupping again.

"It's okay, you big lush."

"Hey there's one of them lock thingy's coming up." I observed as I got to my feet and shaded my eyes from the bright sunlight with my hand. "What do we do at a lock?"

"We drive into the little compartment, close the lock gates behind us, then let the water level adjust to the height of the rest of the river. Once we're at the same height as where we're going we open the gates in front of us and sail through."

"Sounds simple enough." I slurred agreeably.

It did sound simple, and it should have been simple...but it wasn't.

***

"Help!" I screamed at the top of my lungs as the barge began to rise up out of the water as the back-end of the boat got caught on the rising lock-gates. "Maaaaxxxx!" I yelled at my oblivious husband who had his back to me as he was winding the lock-gates up, inadvertently raising me and the arse-end of the barge higher and higher up into the air. I grabbed hold of a bit of railing with one hand and my bottle of wine with the other as the front-end of the boat started to dip below the waterline as the back-end rose further into the air. "MAX!" I screamed again.

After what seemed like an age, Max turned to see his handiwork now that the lock-gate was securely in place. He had been about to reassure me that we simply had to wait now for the lock to fill up so that we could be on our way; instead he was greeted by the sight of a half sunk, half flying barge

-with his drunken wife clinging onto the back of it for dear life. As I struggled for purchase with my feet against the slippery stern, I lost one of my bloody stupid boat shoes into the water below.

Yes, I freely admit that it was my fault. But, in my defence I wasn't the one who brought the alcohol aboard and I wasn't the one who kept filling my glass up to the brim every five minutes. It's also not my fault that in my inebriated state, I was put in charge of guiding the barge into the lock whilst Max attended to the lock gates; he knows parking is *not* my forte. I *also* must make this point clear – *I am not a professional sailor!*

A couple of hours later -and after a hefty bribe to the lock keeper- the barge was once again horizontal and afloat. Fortunately, the barge hadn't taken on water. Although the front-end had been underwater, most of the front-end was water-tight with the hatches closed. The interior was a mess though, as everything that had *been* loose in there *had* come loose in there. Plus, our marriage had sunk into the deep, dark, depths, once again.

"Do you want a cup of tea?" I asked Max, proffering a cup at him. He was sitting on the back of the barge, driving us along at a much quicker pace than before, in stony silence.

He pointedly ignored me and kept his eyes on the river ahead.

"I said I'm sorry." I offered.

His eyebrows shot up involuntarily for a moment before resuming their previous cross position.

"I didn't do it on purpose. It could have happened to anyone."

"But it never *does* happen to anyone else does it?" He snapped. "It's *always* you!"

I didn't have an answer for that.

In a softer voice he added, "Just leave me for a bit will you? Just let me calm down?"

"Okay." I nodded and started climbing carefully back below. "But I am sorry."

"I know." He said with a sigh.

***

By the time he'd moored us up and come back down the ladder into the cabin, his mood had improved a little.

"I'm still sorry." I told him as I set the little table in readiness of our meal.

"And I still know." He retorted. Though despite the seriousness of his tone there was a little more humour in his eyes now.

"Are you hungry?"

"Actually, I'm starving."

I then laid out the supposedly *romantic meal* I had been preparing for the last hour. As romantic meals go -it was a bit of a let-down. I had meant to cook us *chicken fricassee*, which was Max's favourite, but unfortunately it went wrong. The white sauce the chicken was supposed to be cooked in didn't thicken and just stayed like milk.

Max stared down at the dish in front of him and dipped his spoon into the milk before raising it to his face and looking puzzled.

"It went a bit wrong." I offered.

He stared at the milk on his spoon for a moment before starting to laugh, a slow, tired- *can this day get any worse?* - kind of laugh. He let the spoon drop into the dish with a bang.

"I tell you what," I said getting to my feet, "let's go find a pub. There's bound to be one around here somewhere."

"Go on then." He said with a tired half-smile.

***

We queued up at the bar of a little pub we found not far from the river. It seemed quite a nice jolly place with a pleasant atmosphere - but more importantly – they did food.

Max stood next to me at the bar looking despondent as I waved a ten pound note in the air to attract the barmaid's attention. He looked so sad just standing there that I decided to take matters into my own hands and cheer him up a little. It would take me well out of my comfort zone, but then again, that's why I've been having therapy isn't it?

When the barmaid who was serving me asked if I was local, I found myself telling her yes, yes I was. Max looked up with a start as I introduced myself.

"My name is Dolly, and this is my husband Clint." I said gesturing to a bewildered Max.

"So, have you just moved into the area?" She asked as she pulled Max's pint.

"Yes, just moved in today."

She put the pint down onto the drip-tray with a smile. "I bet I know who you are, I bet you're that couple who bought that old manor house out on Beck Lane!"

"Guilty." I said with a laugh. I felt Max squeeze my hand in confusion. I squeezed it back, in what I thought was a *trust me* gesture.

She was eyeing us now with a new curiosity. "You're very brave taking that place on you know."

I waved my hand nonchalantly. "Oh, we like a challenge, don't we darling."

"Oh...yes...Dolly."

I offered the barmaid my money but she waved it away. "On the house loves. God knows you're gonna need your Dutch courage if you're sleeping there tonight."

Intriguing! I thought.

After ordering and eating a big meal, Max had coloured up a little and looked much more relaxed lying his arse off, regaling the locals with tales of what we intended to do with the manor we just bought.

"My wife and I are newly married." Max bragged. "Still in the honeymoon phase... if you know what I mean." He then grabbed my bottom making me jump. Woah there pal, I thought.

I fixed my face and stayed in character. "Yes, the manor is a wedding present."

One of the locals sidled over. "That'd not be a wedding present I'd be glad of; I tell ya!"

"Shhh Larry." The barmaid scolded him. "Don't go scaring them with stupid ghost stories. It's nothing but nonsense anyway." She shook her head at us apologetically.

Max was well into his stride by now. "The only thing going bump-in-the-night is going to be me and the wife!" -Which was met by much sniggering from the elderly men around us.

The locals were very friendly -or nosey depending on how you look at it, and wanted to know everything about their new neighbours. By the time the last bell had rung, Max and I were blotto, and so when we were asked if we wanted to stay for a *lock-in* -what with us being locals now, we thought that was a grand idea. Then out came the *special* whisky.

The last hour that we were there is a little hazy in both Max's and my memories. We have tried remembering more of the last hour but the memories seem buried beneath many layers of that *special whisky.* I do have a faint recollection of waking up after the ground beneath me started bumping, before being shushed and told to go back to sleep. Before I passed out again I had the distinct impression that I was being transported across fields.

It was some hours later when I woke up properly. It was very dark and I could hear a faint noise off in the distance. As my tired brain tried to work out what the noise was, I felt something touch my foot. I woke up properly then with a start. There was a very, very faint light very far above me which gave me just enough light to see Max laid next to me. I rubbed at my tired head and thought about it. If Max was at the side of me, who was touching my foot? I froze as my eyes adjusted enough to see a pair of yellow eyes staring down at me - billows of steam coming from its snout as it stamped its cloven hoof menacingly at me.

"Aghhhh!" I screamed as I shot to my feet. "Max! Max! Wake up! Monster, Max, there's a monster!"

He opened his eyes puzzled before they went wide and he yelped, leaping to his feet beside me. As our eyes accustomed to the dark around us we realised that the monster before us was a large curious sheep.

"What the hell?" Asked Max scratching his head.

"I don't know!" I yelled in a panic. "I just woke up!"

"Where are we?"

"I don't know, but I don't like it!" As I looked up, I realised the faint light I had seen was the full moon, shining through the broken rafters of a roof.

I started to cry as the sheep lifted its tail and proceeded to urinate on my open-toe sandals.

***

By the time the sun came up we realised that we must have passed out in the pub, and so the locals had *kindly* brought us home to 'our' derelict manor -in a wheelbarrow, to sleep in the straw, amongst the sheep that had made the old ruins their home. How kind!

I pulled a lump of straw out of my hair and fished my handbag out of one of the wheelbarrows that were parked up next to us before we set off in search of our narrowboat.

***

The next night we spent together was on the barge, after a much more pleasant day. And...I am surprised to report that I well and truly came out from under my bridge after all!

Max said 'it' happened because we'd bonded over a shared hardship -and there might be something to that. After waking up in the middle of the night, in the middle of nowhere, face to face with an angry sheep we believed was a monster, it was nice to cuddle up together in the cosy cabin, locking out the rest of the world for a while.

Plus, in my defence, it was actually Dolly and Clint that did 'it'.

Chapter Twenty-Eight

"What are you grinning at?" TLS enquired the following day when we returned home.

"I don't know what you're talking about?" I answered innocently.

He cocked his horns at me suspiciously. "Hm. Never mind, I don't think I want to know."

I shrugged indifferently and carried on unpacking with a silly smile on my face that I was struggling to shake off. With great deliberation I picked my Sudoku book up from off my bedside table and discarded it into the pedal bin in the corner of my bedroom.

As I put away my suitcase I noticed something glittering in the sunlight just beneath the bed. Puzzled, I got down on my hands and knees and peered under my valence sheet. "What the hell?"

As I reached my hand under the bed I realised that what I was looking at was one of Lola's earrings. It made my stomach sink for a moment as I turned it over in my hand. For a while I'd managed to put her to the back of my memory, but here I held in my hand a little memento, testament to her affair with my husband. It made me feel cold.

My sudden happy mood had vanished in the blink of a diamante earing. With a flick of my wrist I flung the cursed thing into the pedal bin and sat down on the bed to think, before sharply getting to my feet as the memory of Lola and Max -in that bed - burst into my brain. What had I been *thinking* going along with this whole '*giving it another go*' lark? I was being a fool wasn't I?

I shuddered involuntarily as I thought of the previous evening's shenanigans. Well if nothing else it had made my mind up for me at last. That was it. I deserved better than this...didn't I?

I pulled the suitcase back out and began to pack.

***

I dragged the suitcase down the stairs once TLS had gone out, I didn't want him to see it and get upset. I'd sit him down and try and explain everything to him later on. With a groan I picked up the kitchen phone and dialled my mother's number. I wasn't looking forward to the phone call but I had to give her notice about needing a bed. While it rang I reached out to the fridge magnets that spelled out 'nipples' and changed them to 'tipples'.

"Hello?" Barked the angry voice.

"Mum, it's me."

"Who?"

"Your daughter."

"Have you got rid of that bloody Polish man yet? If not, I have nothing to say to you."

"Wrong daughter." I banged my head against the cupboard door quietly. "Look Mum, have you got a spare room for a few days?"

"Oh, it's you. Why? Has Max chucked you out?"

"No Mum…"

"You haven't done anything else stupid have you? Not got yourself into another bloody scrape?"

"No, nothing like that. Look…"

"Have you gone and got yourself arrested?"

"Not yet, but it's looking more and more likely." I snapped back. How long would I get for committing matricide? I wonder if it's worth finding out?

"You can't have my spare room anyway. I'm already renting it out."

"To who?"

"To whom."

"Okay, to whom?"

"A strange little fellow called John. The local florist recommended him as a good tenant. To be honest I'm not finding it to be a very suitable arrangement. I have a terrible feeling that he might be one of those."

"One of those what?" I asked cringing.

"You know, a bit…exuberant. Wears flowery shirts; talks a lot about his mother, has a manicure. Likes…"

"Willies?"

"Claire!"

"What?"

"Don't be so vulgar."

"Don't be so homophobic." I was starting to see how *stupid* I had been even *thinking* about living with that woman.

"Don't take that tone with me. I am your mother!"

"Are you?"

"What's that supposed to mean?"

"I might have been mixed up at birth." I crossed my fingers, I could always hope. "I always rather fancied that I might belong to some other family."

"How *dare* you!"

"Oh I'm like that old SAS motto Mum.... I dare."

The dial tone assaulted my eardrum as she put the phone down on me. Oh well, whoever poor John was, I bet he was regretting renting a room from my mother.

I remember being about six years old and getting angry with my mother for her nasty comments about people on TV. I stormed into the kitchen to tell my dad that my mummy was both a racist (I'd learnt that word at school) and a *poofist*! I couldn't understand why my dad was rolling around laughing at me, every now and then coming up for air and gasping the word '*poofist*' before howling with laughing again.

It wasn't my fault. I was six, I'd never heard of the word homophobic before, so I'd improvised.

Chapter Twenty-Nine

"You've never mentioned your father before." The therapist observed thoughtfully.

I shrugged. "I haven't seen him for a long time so I don't tend to think of him much."

"Why haven't you seen him for a long time? You mentioned previously that your parents had a difficult divorce. Was that a contributing factor?"

"Definitely. My mother wouldn't let him keep in touch with us."

"Why was that?"

"Because he changed his name, bought a tambourine and joined a cult."

She sat up with a start. "Your father joined a cult?"

"Yes, why?"

"And you never thought to mention it?"

"Why would I? It was a long time ago."

She slapped her forehead. "It never occurred to you that the problem you have with organised religion might have something to do with your father leaving you and joining a cult?"

I pondered it a while.

She sat shaking her head at me in silence. I was

also quite surprised to note that she had developed a twitch in her eye not unlike my own. Why did she feel the need to make me feel like an idiot? I'm not an idiot.

Once her twitch was back under control she got back to business as usual. "Was your father religious before he joined the cult or was his religiousness a product of the cult?"

"He was always quite religious. Marched us up to the church every Sunday, made us read the bible and say prayers and the like."

"Where was your mother while this was going on? I take it that she wasn't a party to religion due to her, er...lack of...generosity of spirit?"

"Oh quite the opposite. They were both devout Christians back then. My mum doesn't really bother anymore, but back then, oh yes. Thinking about it, that's probably why I've always had a problem with religion. My parents were two of the most unkind, ungenerous, uncharitable people you could ever meet, yet they believed that just because they went to church regularly, somehow they were morally superior to everyone else. It's always really bothered me."

"Why Claire," She said, suddenly smiling dementedly, "I believe you've had a breakthrough."

"I have?"

"You have."

"Okay."

"So what happened after you phoned your

mum?"

"Ah," this was better, I could get back on track now. "Well it clarified for me that I categorically cannot go live with my mother."

"So...."

"So I decided to be brave and have a talk with Max and tell him how upset I'd been about the earring."

She clapped her hands together with delight. "That is *excellent* news. Facing things head on, that's what I've been waiting to see. Why, I'm stunned. I was starting to think that we were going to go around in circles forever, but I'm actually seeing a real improvement. Well done!" She was grinning at me like a maniac. Gosh she had a lot of teeth!

"Thanks." Wow, a compliment? I was starting to feel quite bad for secretly comparing her head to a snow globe.

"So, go on then, how did the talk with Max go?"

"Oh, it didn't. I unpacked my suitcase, got on with making our tea and by the time Max came home I had decided to keep my mouth shut, put the earring out of my mind, and resolved not to rock the boat."

She stared at me for ages, as though she was trying to telekinetically make my head explode like that man off the film 'Scanners'. I also didn't like the way she was starting to rake her nails through her scalp, looking as though a handful of her frizzy hair was going to be departing any moment.

"So let me get this straight," she said finally as she pulled some loose hair from her bitten fingertips, "since I saw you last, you began impersonating Dolly Parton, caused a potential terrorist situation, sank a barge, and was urinated on by a sheep; yet the idea of discussing finding your husband's tart's earring with him is a step too far?"

"You said the T word." I pointed out.

"What?" She spluttered.

"Tart. You said it was offensive, but you just said it."

I looked away as her sudden twitching was making me feel uncomfortable. Out of the two of us, she looked far more in need of psychological help than I did. In fact, the more time I spent in her company the more she seemed to unravel. When I first met her she seemed very professional and very...together. Now, she looked a complete nervous wreck.

I wasn't entirely sure at first, but I thought she might have started to hum under her breath. I listened carefully to her with my head cocked on one side. She *was* humming - and rocking very slightly. The tune she was humming sounded quite familiar to me. What was it? Eventually the penny dropped and I realised she was humming the theme music from the film *Rocky*. I was a little baffled and didn't know what to do as she seemed very absorbed in it, so after a while I thought the best thing to do was to join in.

I wasn't that familiar with all of the words in '*Eye of the tiger*,' but I knew the tune well enough to hum along.

As we reached the crescendo of the chorus together– '*and he's watching us all with the eye…. of the tiger.*' –she finally stopped humming and spoke in a strange robotic sounding tone. "I think we'll leave this session there for now."

I had been about to start humming the next verse when she left me hanging, making me feel stupid. "Oh, okay." I looked at the clock, we still had ten minutes to go. "I'll see you next week then." I said, getting to my feet.

"I don't think so. I think I might be…having some more time off."

"Okay."

Chapter Thirty

"Hello Jean." I greeted the old homeless lady as I approached her. "I thought I'd bring you a little treat up today."

She took a step back as I approached her.

"Here." I offered her a big parcel that contained an 'all terrain' sleeping bag that I had just purchased from an army supply store in town. I don't know why I hadn't thought of it before. I'd brought her old sleeping bags and blankets before, but an army one would have to be better wouldn't it? At least it would be waterproof. So what if she looked like an OAP paratrooper? At least she'd be warm.

"Ta." She said taking the bundle from my arms suspiciously.

"Is there anything else you need before I go?"

She looked at me curiously for a moment. "Why do you look after me?"

"Guilt." I answered truthfully.

She raised her eyebrows as though I'd made perfect sense, before turning her back to me and unpacking the bundle. I understood, I was dismissed.

***

It had been a month or so since I had last seen my regular therapist -who had been true to her word with taking time off. The other locum therapists that I had seen didn't really seem very interested in me anyway and thought that I didn't need therapy. (To which I concurred.) They just went through the motions as it was state appointed sessions.

I was feeling much better anyway. Max and I did end up having the earring talk after all. He was very sympathetic and apologetic, and even went out the very same day and bought us a new bed – which really did make me feel better.

Whilst I was out in town today he was home redecorating the bedroom too. A fresh start and all that. In fact, *that* was one of the reasons I was out of the house and playing for time. I knew full well if I went home I would get roped into helping with the decorating – and that is never a good idea. Me and emulsion paint don't get on very well, although it seems to get on me very well.

The other reason for being out of the house was that I had a secret.

***

Once I was home and I had ascertained that the decorating was done and I wouldn't have to help, (hinder) I slipped the paper parcel out of my handbag sneakily and began tiptoeing towards the stairs.

"Claire!" Max bellowed, making me jump and hide the parcel up my jumper before he could see it.

"Yes?"

"I said do you want a brew? Didn't you hear me calling you?"

"Oh, sorry I didn't hear you. Yes, I will have one please." I then gave him my best leave me alone smile. He seemed pacified by it and trotted off rolling his eyes.

Once I was satisfied that he'd gone, I retrieved my parcel from up my jumper and headed upstairs.

I sat on the toilet and pulled the leaflet out of the little box to read the instructions.

"Okay, so this end I wee on." I mumbled under my breath as I pulled a cap off one end of the little stick. I went back to the instructions which had lots of little pictures of blue lines and crosses. "I don't even know why I'm doing this." I told the instructions. "It can't possibly be positive."

**

I don't know how long I sat there on the toilet staring in disbelief at the little blue cross that had popped up in the little window at the end of the stick. "How could this happen?" I whispered. "I can't do this...I'm too old for this."

I didn't matter how much I concentrated on it, that little blue cross just wouldn't disappear.

"Oh God!" I shook my head at the little stick. "What the hell do I do now?"

There would be no getting rid of it, (the baby I mean, not the stick) that wasn't something that I could even consider. The stick however, I *would* be hiding until I could pluck up the courage to tell Max. Oh God, and Paul! He'd think this was hilarious! Oh no!

I spent the rest of the afternoon avoiding Max and Paul as much as possible. Fortunately, they were used to my odd behaviour so they didn't go quizzing me too much.

Once I finally had the house to myself I decided that I might need some help or advice or something as I was quietly freaking out. I decided to call Carly as she seemed to be quite calm and unflappable -which was just what I needed. I paced up and down impatiently as her phone rang and rang before finally putting me through to her voice mail. "Shit!" I told the *beep* before hanging up. I tried a few more people before biting the bullet and calling my sister Rachel. As I have said before, my sister and I aren't very close and tend to only see each other at special occasions. It's not that we don't get on or anything like that, it's just that we don't have anything in common. While I am the 'wimpy one' as Rachel puts it, she is the brave one, a take-no-shit, assertive modern woman. I annoy her.

I was almost disappointed when she answered the phone straight away. "Hello?"

"Rachel? It's me, Claire."

"Oh God what's happened?"

"What do you mean?"

"Is it Mum? Has she pegged it?"

I shook my head at the phone in annoyance. "Not yet but I'm working on it."

"Oh." She sounded a little disappointed I thought. "So what's up then? Is everything okay?"

"I'm pregnant."

"Shut up! You're not?" She sounded like she was trying not to laugh which quite got my back up.

"Afraid so."

"I can't believe it. You're too old to have a baby. What does Max think? Is it Max's baby? Last time I saw Mum she said she thought Max was getting sick of you moping around and that you'd probably end up getting divorced."

The twitch was making a reappearance in my right eye. "Of course it's Max's, he just doesn't know yet, and no I don't think we will be getting divorced, especially not now."

"Oh I see," she said knowingly, "have you got pregnant on purpose? To keep Max?"

"Piss off."

"I'll take that as a no."

I decided to change the subject before I could lose my temper with her. "So are you getting serious with the Polish fella then?"

"What Polish fella?"

"Mum said you were going out with a Polish fella and that she'd disowned you over it."

She started laughing. "That was the plumber who answered the door when she came around. I was thinking on my feet when I introduced him as my boyfriend. I knew it'd drive her nuts and get her off my back for a bit. He played along with it while he was fixing my boiler."

"Oh. Damn, I wish I could've thought of something like that."

"It was definitely one of my finer moments."

"I thought your best moment was when she fell asleep soaking her feet in her foot spa..."

She interrupted me. "Yeah and I poured in a bag of quick-setting cement!"

I laughed at the memory. That was the incident that got her thrown out of the house at sixteen. "It was so funny. I don't know how you dared. It took me ages to chip her out of the damned thing with a hammer and chisel after you left."

We found ourselves giggling for a while at the memory of our mother sat in her *Shackleton's* armchair with her feet set in cement in a whirlpool foot spa.

"So what are you going to do then? About the baby?"

"I don't know. I'm frightened to death. I'm keeping it though, that much I do know."

"How far along are you?"

"Not very long. Six weeks maybe? I need to go to doctors and get it confirmed."

She said a little more gently - "Do you want me to

come with you?"

"Would you?"

"If you want me to."

"I think I'd like that if you don't mind."

"Well it'll give us a chance to catch up won't it."

I breathed a sigh of relief. "I've got quite a lot to tell you."

Chapter Thirty-One

"I don't like this." I whispered to Rachel as we sat in the waiting room of my local GP. "That bloody receptionist keeps glaring at me. Stuck-up cow, who does she think she is?"

"They're all like that aren't they." She replied. "Self-important twits who seem to think that they know more than the doctors do."

I nodded my approval at her answer. I was secretly pleased to have my sister here with me. I really hoped her assertiveness might rub off on me a little bit. I was surprised how supportive she was being, as I normally drove her up the wall. To say she was my little sister, anyone who didn't know us would have surely thought her to be the elder sister; she's so much more confident and self-assured than I am.

"Why don't you take that lemon out of your mouth love!" Rachel bellowed across the room to the receptionist who had been glaring at us since I had refused to tell her the reason for my visit with the doctor.

I had made an appointment to see a doctor, not to have my private medical business dissected in front of a room full of other patients, by a woman - who when she isn't working here, works part-time on the meat counter in *Tesco.* I don't think so!

"So what are you going to call it?" Rachel asked, breaking me from my thoughts.

"I don't know; I haven't thought about it."

"You ought to give it a really cool first name, and then a horrendous middle name just for a laugh. You know, something to torture it with when it turns into an arsey teenager."

I looked at her worriedly. "It's going to be an arsey teenager one day isn't it? Oh Jesus, I thought I was almost done with arsey teenagers!"

She sniggered under her breath, she was enjoying my discomfort far too much. "Just think about it, you've only had experience of an arsey teenage boy, what if you have an arsey teenage girl?"

"Oh shit!"

"You'd have to have the sex talk, period talk, teach her that boys are arseholes..."

"Stop it!" I was having palpitations. "A girl would *have* to be easier. Do you have any idea of the *things* I have accidently seen Paul doing? Oh God the things I've seen." I covered my eyes with my hand in an effort to try and erase the offending images from my brain. "And the smells! His bedroom smells like nothing on earth!"

"Did Mum ever have the period talk with you?" she asked.

I frowned. "The closest she ever came to it was

when I found her tampons and asked her what they were. She said she'd borrowed them from the little family that lived next door who used them as draft excluders."

She chuckled. "God she was horrible to that little family wasn't she."

"Do you remember her telling you the dad next door was the tooth fairy?"

"Yeah." She said with obvious embarrassment.

"Anyway," I said, getting back to the point, "a girl has to be easier than a boy."

"Girls are meaner though."

"Girls are lovely compared to boys."

She pulled a wry face at me. "Do you remember what we were like as teenagers? We were horrible. For Christ sake, I set our mum in concrete just so she couldn't stop me going to an Oasis concert! And you weren't much better."

"What did I do?"

"You gave away her fur coat to the salvation army!"

"Did I? I don't remember that."

"Okay maybe that was me." She conceded. "But you did stuff too."

Did I? I certainly didn't remember. I was too terrified of our mother to dare do anything to antagonise her.

"Oo I know what you did."

"What did I do?"

Her eyes lit up with excitement. "You put laxatives in her Horlicks!"

I shook my head sadly. "No, that was still you."

"Really?" She looked disappointed and sat back with a sigh. "So you really never got your own back on Mum?"

"Nope. I was too scared of her."

"Don't take this the wrong way, but you seem different now. You don't seem so...timid. To be honest you used to drive me crazy, but now...not so much."

"Thank you, I think. I do *get* what you mean. I know I'm not very brave but I am trying harder since I was sectioned. My therapist says..."

She butted in loudly, "You were sectioned?"

"Shush." I looked about me to see if she'd been overheard. "Didn't Mum tell you?"

"We don't talk anymore. How the hell did you get sectioned?"

I became aware of the snotty receptionist leaning closer towards us trying to eavesdrop. "I'll tell you later." I then gestured with my head towards the nosey receptionist who suddenly seemed fascinated with the poster above my head.

"You better!" She replied.   "So.... baby names then?" I asked in an effort to change the subject. She sat staring at me for a moment before shaking her head and moving on. "Okay! Well, I think you should call it – if it's a boy – Harley, or maybe Levi. You know, something tough and cool like that. Then for a middle name, Hillary or something stupid and girly like that!"

I laughed despite myself. Paul would have been devastated if his middle name was Hillary. I snorted. "What if it's a girl though?"

She thought about it for a moment. "Mm, again a really cool first name..."

"Such as?"

"I don't know; girls' names are hard aren't they? Anyway, same as before, cool first name, hideous second name. Do you remember the name of the girl in that film we used to love when we were little -*Swallows and Amazons?*"

I did. "I'm not calling my daughter Titty!"

"Oh go on, just for a laugh."

"Bugger off."

I was grateful when the buzzer went off that indicated it was my turn for the doctor. Titty indeed!

***

"You're what?" Max exclaimed the following day when I broke the news to him.

"Pregnant, up the duff, got a bun in the oven."

He sank down onto the sofa with a bump. The shock was apparent by his paling face and shaking hands. "Seriously?"

I nodded.

"Wow." He said quietly. "I just thought you were getting a bit fat."

"Hey!" I exclaimed. "There's no need for the F word! I'm not even far along enough to show yet." I peered around to try and see my bottom in a panic. Fat? Me?

"I was joking." He said smiling weakly. "Sorry it's just my defence mechanism kicking in."

I tutted whilst slyly feeling my bottom discretely just to make sure he was joking.

"How do you feel about it?" He asked.

"Shocked at first. It's going to get some getting used to." I sat down next to him and put my feet up on the coffee table with a sigh.

"You know what?" He said, turning to me. "This might be just what we need."

"Seriously?"

"Yeah. It's like a second chance isn't it. A real opportunity to start again, turn over a new leaf; and this time, we won't mess it up." He punctuated this with a kiss to my hand.

I found myself smiling back and getting caught up in the moment. "So you don't mind?"

"Mind? It's a shock, but I think it's the best news we could've got."

Wow!

"Who's going to tell Paul?" I asked.

"Oh please let me? I want to see his face when I tell him the baby's sharing his bedroom."

"You rotten bugger!" I smiled and rested my head against his shoulder. "Hey, wait a minute, where the hell are we going to put the baby? The spare room's tiny, there isn't room to swing a cat in there."

"How do you feel about moving house?"

I gasped. "I'd love to move house! I hate this house."

"So do I. If we're having a fresh start and all that, why don't we move and make it a proper fresh start? New house, new baby, new life."

"Can we afford it?"

"We can't afford a mansion or anything, but we can definitely get something a little bit bigger."

I was so happy I could burst!

Chapter Thirty-Two

I was sitting in the little waiting area outside my therapist's office when the urge to wee drove me into the ladies' toilets. I was only six months pregnant but this little bundle of joy was squatting heavily on my bladder making me virtually incontinent, just to add a little more joy to my life!

I resented having to still come to these ridiculous sessions as my regular therapist had disappeared after the 'eye of the tiger' session, and none of the locums seemed interested in anything other than banal chit-chat. Still, at least I only had one more session after this one.

As I exited the cubicle and wandered over to the sink to wash my hands, I heard the toilet next to mine flush. Looking up in the mirror I was astounded to see my old therapist coming towards me. She still looked a little frazzled but at least she wasn't twitching quite as much as the last time I saw her. That is until our eyes met in the mirror. As I smiled at her she burst out with something under her breath that sounded somewhat like - "Holy Mary, mother of God!"

"So you're back then I see." I remarked pleasantly.

She stared at me a moment. "So you're still here?"

"Only one more session after this one then I'm out of here forever!"

She carried on staring at me and began absent-mindedly twirling her hair around her fingers nervously. "So one day you *will* leave?"

I was a little confused by her behaviour. Maybe she was having an *off* day? I pretended not to notice. "I'm sorry I'm here a little early. I don't mind waiting for a while until it's my proper appointment time."

"You're fat!" She suddenly declared pointedly.

"Pregnant!" I told her proudly.

She stared down at her hands pointedly as she began to wash them furiously in the sink in front of her.

"I'm six months gone."

She nodded and carried on scrubbing her hands.

"Well, erm, I'll be waiting outside then." I offered awkwardly.

She never replied and so I left the ladies' and returned to my seat outside to wait for her. It seemed to take ages for her to come out, and when she did finally show her face, to my surprise she sat down next to me in the waiting room. She didn't speak to me, but just stared straight ahead as if I wasn't even there. Strange.

I was just opening my mouth to break the silence when the office door opened and the locum therapist -whom I had seen previously- shouted, "Madeleine?"

"Yes!" Shouted my therapist, leaping to her feet and hurrying through the office door as quickly as she could before slamming the door behind her.

I was more than a little puzzled. Was there a staff meeting going on?

I think I sat for around ten minutes counting the tiles on the ceiling before I heard my old therapist suddenly shouting on the other side of the door at the top of her lungs.

"I'm telling you, IT WAS THE PUBE IN THE JAM TART!"

Pardon?

Curiosity got the better of me and so I crept towards the door and rested my ear gently against the wood. She was speaking quieter now and so I strained to hear what she was saying.

"Listen to me, I know I sound crazy but hear me out. If she hadn't have found the pube in the jam tart she wouldn't have lost her job, so she wouldn't have been home to be driven around the twist by the Jehovah witnesses, she wouldn't have bought the menorah to deter the Jehovah witnesses, she wouldn't have got herself roped into the Bah mitzvah, never would have given cherry flavour condoms to the Jewish boy- which was the catalyst for the nervous breakdown that led to her scrubbing her husband's tart in the bath at the request of Alan Partridge!"

The other therapist then tried to interrupt her

without success.

"And if all that hadn't happened, I would never have had that woman in my office every week driving me around the twist! She's ruined my life! I used to take comfort in religion in times of stress, now, thanks to her, I can't see the image of Jesus without picturing him in a Santa suit! I can't *tell* her anything, because it just goes in one ear and out the other! For *weeks* we discussed why she might have a problem with religion and not once in all those sessions did she make the connection that *maybe* her problem with religion comes from the fact that her father ran off and joined a cult!"

Ouch! I wasn't sure that I wanted to hear anymore but I found that my body was disobeying me and was forcing my ear back against the door.

"She's even got me using the word TART!" She paused for a moment. "And now, she's out *there*, pregnant! Pregnant to the man that she hates! I bet that wouldn't have happened if not for the pube in the jam tart too!"

She went quiet for a moment and I was considering leaving the building and going home, but it turned out she wasn't done.

"She impersonates Dolly Parton you know. While she was dressed as Dolly Parton - in a burka, she caused a terrorist situation due to her tits being mistaken for semtex!"

"I think you need to calm down now Madeleine." I heard the therapist say. "You know as well as I do that there are difficult patients out there who need a little more help than others. You can't take their problems personally."

"Take it personally? She's ruined my life!"

I thought that was very uncalled for. I stared at the door in disgust.

I heard the therapist interrupt again. "Have you tried the theme song that you picked to help you out when you get distressed?"

"I tried that!" She exclaimed. "She bloody joined in with me! We were both sat there rocking and humming *the eye of the bastard tiger* together!"

"Can you please lower your voice Madeleine?"

"No. No I can't. I won't. I SAID I WON'T!" She bellowed.

"I think it's best to end this session for today, we'll resume again next week." I heard the therapist say tiredly.

I made my way back over to the seating area and sat back down quickly, trying to digest the conversation I had heard. After a moment, the door clicked open and Madeleine came slinking out making a point of not looking over at me. I was more than a little confused. Was this a test? Were they in on it together? Or, did my therapist finally understand the significance of the jam tart? I decided to be brave and took a stab in the dark.

"So you see now?" I called to her.

She blew her nose and turned her teary eyes to me.

"It's the pube in the jam tart. It all comes back to that."

She nodded quietly.

"And now it's got a second victim hasn't it?"

She nodded.

"It'll all come right in the end." I told her.

She sniffed. "What do you mean?"

"Everything happens for a reason. I can't say it's God because I don't believe in him, but maybe it's fate. I went through hell after the pube incident, but now...gosh I'm so glad it happened. It changed my life. At first for the worst, admittedly, but now, now my life's wonderful."

"Really? You really think that?"

"I do." I said stroking my belly. "I've never been happier."

She stared at me a moment longer before offering me a sad smile and leaving.

I was suddenly very aware of being stared at. I turned to see the locum therapist standing in the doorway. "Do you want to come through Claire?"

Chapter Thirty-Three

I had been thinking all day about my poor therapist. I felt awful for her. I knew full well how fast a life could unravel by a chance twist of fate. I could only hope that fate had something better in store for her.

She may think that I hadn't been listening to her, but I really have. I must have mustn't I? Look at how much my life had turned around since being in therapy. I'm now happily married again with a baby on the way; Max has put an offer in on a house that we both love, and we've just accepted full asking price on our own house. Plus, I even have a job again! As Lola had been transferred to a different building, her old job was up for grabs...so I grabbed it. I spend my days now doing the odd bit of filing and gossiping with my friends Carly and Stephanie, in between helping Max look for his 'stapler' in the stationary cupboard.

I even have my sister back, who thankfully can stand to be around me now. She thinks my nervous breakdown is the funniest thing that she's ever heard and thinks it would make a good book. But, who would believe me?

***

"Hey Hun." Carly said as I sat back down at my desk.

"Hey." I smiled back.

"How did therapy go?"

"Shit. I think I broke my therapist."

She laughed and shook her head at me before returning to her paperwork. Didn't she realise I was being serious? I busied myself with the stack of papers that had been left on my desk to file.

My phone suddenly started ringing, startling me a little.

"Hello?"

"Am I speaking to Claire?"

"Yes."

"Claire Porter?"

"Yes." I said again getting impatient.

"How are you today?"

Oh for the good old days when I could have perhaps shared with him the discomfort of my haemorrhoids. Instead I grated my teeth before replying – "Fine thanks."

"Good, good." - Came the false laugh. "I'm calling from *Stationary Wares*; can I interest you in any office supplies today? We have a special offer on printer ink and...."

"Whoa, let me stop you there," I interrupted, "we don't need any office supplies today thank you. We already have our own supplier that we're happy with thank you."

"I'm sure we can offer you a much more competitive quote. How much do you pay per unit for envelopes?"

"I said, no thank you. We already have our own supplier."

"And who is that supplier madam if you don't mind me asking?"

"I do mind you asking and how dare you call me madam, I may have a slightly feminine voice but that doesn't mean you have the right to call me by the wrong gender." I crossed my fingers and caught Carly's eye – who had started laughing at me. I winked back before continuing. "Claire is short for Clarence!"

Carly gave an involuntary snort.

"I am ever so sorry Claire, erm Clarence. I do apologise."

"I should think so!"

Carly was sniggering behind her monitor as I finally put the phone down with a bang. Yes, I might have acted childish, but maybe that's not such a bad thing. I find these days that just a little bit of venting stops the pressure cooker in my brain building up too much.

"That was genius." Carly said as she came across and sat on the edge of my desk.

"It tickled me." I replied grinning.

She shook her blonde wigged head at me. "I love

having you here. You always cheer me up."

"Thanks."

"Any-who, I have news."

I perked up. "Oh yes?"

"I have my date."

"Date?" It took a moment for the penny to drop. "Oh the date for your op? Wow! When is it?"

She pulled a nervous smile. "May the sixth."

"God. That's only three months away!"

"I know! I don't know whether to be excited or terrified!"

"Excited. You have to be. I know it'll take a lot of recovery, but I'm sure you won't regret it."

"Hope not. It's not like they can sew it back on if I change my mind."

"Can you keep it?"

"It doesn't work like that."

"I don't know much about the...logistics of it." I admitted.

She looked about her cautiously. After ascertaining that Max was nowhere to be seen, she proceeded to load up YouTube on my computer. "Watch this!" She ordered as she typed in 'sex change operation'.

"Oh my good God!" I cried putting my hands over my eyes as the scalpel started flying. "I can't watch."

"At least you don't have to go through it."

"I'd rather go through it than watch it being done! Jesus that's horrible. Why would they put someone's operation on YouTube?"

"It's informative."

"It's bloody gruesome."

"You see now why I'm nervous?"

I nodded. "I think you're amazingly brave."

"Thanks." She paused a moment. "Hey, we'll both be in hospital at the same time won't we? Isn't that round about your due date?"

"It is."

"Just think," she said smirking, "we'll both be in there having something removed from our privates."

"Mm."

Chapter Thirty-Four

I trudged up my garden path, past the sold sign and around the puddles of water that had built up since the previous day's rain storm. As I put my key in the lock I winced at the loud rock music coming from TLS's bedroom. I shook my head at the ceiling in despair.

With great relief, I pulled off my soggy shoes and left them on top of the radiator in the hall to dry out before dropping my key onto the hook on the wall next to the door.

I tried for a moment to work out what the hell that racket upstairs was. Nirvana maybe? Foo Fighters? I didn't care. I walked over to the fuse box and flicked it to OFF. Blessed silence reigned once again.

With a self-satisfied smile I got my whistling kettle out of the cupboard and filled it with water before setting it onto the gas stove. Once the kettle was on the go, I sat down on the sofa and got comfy.

After a few moments I heard TLS come thundering down the stairs in a temper.

"Power cut!" He bellowed at me.

"Nope. Privilege cut." I retorted with a smile.

"What?"

"Unplug your speakers and I'll turn the electric back on."

"What?" - Said his gormless face again.

"You heard me. If you won't listen to your music at an appropriate level, you won't listen to it at all!"

"You could just have told me to turn it down, you didn't have to turn the bloody leccy off." He snapped.

"So if I'd have burst into your room just now to tell you to turn it down, you wouldn't have been in the middle of masturbating?"

"Mum!" He spluttered, his cheeks flushing.

I pointed at him calmly. "If *I* have to be embarrassed by *your* masturbating then you should be too. The Catholics might be on to something with that. Now go unplug them bloody speakers and get your homework done!"

He trudged off scowling and muttering under his breath.

Don't you just love being in control?

***

While Paul was upstairs sulking in silence, I made myself a cup of tea and sat down with the sales brochure for our new home. I was so excited about it that I could virtually reiterate the brochure word-for-word - I had read it so many times. Incidentally, the house was on the same street as

Violet's house, the little old lady with whom I share a bus frequently. Although not as grand as her house, it was still a beautiful period property. Hark at me, *period property*, and getting smugger by the minute! Oh the excitement! Once we get settled in I'm going to have to go and apologise to her for my meltdown on the bus, where I had told her in good faith that I was now Jewish.

The bigger mortgage thing scares me, but then again that's Max's department. He says we can afford it fairly easily since he got a promotion a few months ago. The house isn't huge but there's plenty of room in it for us all -baby included. I just can't wait to get a moving in date now. Hopefully we'll be in before the baby's born.

I rubbed my swollen belly happily. "I wonder what you are little one." I whispered. I hadn't wanted to know the sex of it when I had been offered the chance as I was too frightened that she might tell me I was having a boy. I might well *be* having a boy but at least this way I can pretend for a few months that it is a girl, after all. I tell anyone that asks that I'm having a girl. I'm just hoping that saying off that old film *'The boy who could fly'* might come true. It went something along the lines of – *"Wish long enough and wish hard enough and anything is possible."* I'm counting on it being true. Like I said to my sister, girls must be easier. - They certainly smell better.

I was disturbed from my daydreaming by my

phone suddenly going off in my pocket. I fished it out and squinted at the text message. I didn't like to admit it but my eyesight was starting to go a little bit.

Hey Claire, can you come to mine tomorrow about 4 o clock?
Got something for you. Oooo lol

It was Stephanie. She delighted in spooking me with things, so god only knows what she had in store for me this time. In the last three months I had received similar texts, and on arriving at her flat I had found myself face to face with Anne Summers parties, speed dating (People actually on speed, dating, which was quite a sight to behold!) and the last thing I had been summoned for was a Karaoke party. I live in fear of a microphone being shoved into my face at the best of times, let alone stone-cold-sober in front of a room full of virtual strangers. I uncomfortably fluffed the words through Tina Turner's *Simply the Best* but gave up half way through when people suddenly started departing en masse to the kitchen. I thought I had given it some solid effort so I was slightly peeved at my audience's ingratitude.

The speed dating thing was apparently in my honour as a last ditch attempt to make me see what I was missing out on by staying with Max. In Stephanie's defence, the speed part of it hadn't been her fault. One of the 'gents' she had invited in my honour had 'garnished' the cream cakes with a little sprinkling of his own! Thankfully I was going through horrendous morning sickness at the time and so refrained from the buffet. I just sat bewildered by the blur of people babbling away at me. By the time I managed to escape, (literally, as I shot down the fire escape while they were doing the conga.) they had all decided that I was boring and they should go off to a club to look for some more exciting totty. (Cheers for that.)

As for the Anne Summers party, well the less said about that the better.

With a sigh I shook my head and typed my reply.

Okay, as long as there's no microphones, porn or class A drugs!

I waited for the reply with apprehension. How would she word it so that she could trap me into something stupid?

You know I don't repeat myself! Don't be a wimp, you'll love it this time, I promise!

Just great! What treat would she have in store for me this time?

Chapter Thirty-Five

I huffed and puffed my way up Stephanie's stairs as the lift was broken, thinking all the while – 'please let this not be anything stupid'.

"Hey Claire! Wait up!" A soft brummy accent called out behind me.

"Hi Carly." I exclaimed breathlessly, turning to wait for her to catch up.

She replied, "God I wish they'd hurry up and fix that bloody lift."

"I know." I agreed. "What the hell is Steph up to this time?"

"I've got no idea."

"So you aren't in on this one then?"

She looked puzzled. "No, I just got a text yesterday asking me to come here because she had something for me."

"I got the same text! What's she up to this time?"

"God knows. Come on then," she ordered, "let's be brave and find out."

With anticipation and more than a little dread we made our way up to Steph's flat. As I knocked on the front door I heard Steph hissing on the other side, "Hush!"

Carly and I exchanged a nervous smile.

I heard Steph clear her throat on the other side of the door. "Who is it?"

Carly replied – "Me and Claire."

I heard a lock click open before Steph called, - "It's open. Just let yourselves in!"

After swapping a worried glance, we did a quick game of rock-paper-scissors, which I unfortunately lost.

"Okay then." I said, and opened the door.

We were barely inside when a large group of people with party poppers jumped out at us and yelled "Surprise!"

Surprised? We nearly shat ourselves!

"What's all this in aid of?" I asked as I looked around at all the women holding up pink balloons.

"It's your surprise, well both of your double surprise anyway." Steph replied with a grin. "I got the idea when Carly got her date through yesterday. You're both going into hospital at the same time for something life changing, so I thought I'd throw a baby shower for you Claire and a bon voyage party for your penis Carly. I'm calling it a penis parting party."

I took a sharp intake of breath on Carly's behalf. How would she take this? Wasn't this a little insensitive?

Carly threw her head back and started laughing. She shook her head at Steph. "You're off your head you are. There better be booze at this penis parting party."

"Oh yeah." She pointed Carly over to a little cocktail (no pun intended) bar that had been set up in the corner of her living room.

I looked around nervously at the many people that I barely knew. Some of them I vaguely remembered from the speed-dating-conga-line, and a few people I recognised from work.

After a second glance around I realised that the pink balloons above my head were alternating pink round balloons, and inflatable pink penises. Wait, is that a word? Or is it penii? What is the plural of penis? Anyway, there were a lot of them.

Once Steph had returned from mixing Carly a bizarre looking cocktail she turned to me. "Come on then Claire, let's get you some fruit juice before the games start."

"What games?" I asked worriedly as she lead me off by my elbow.

"We've got pass-the-parcel for you, and a similar game I like to call – 'pass-up-on-the-package' for Carly. That was my idea." She said proudly.

It was a good job Carly had a sense of humour!

To say how crap Steph was at politically correct stuff, she was actually quite thoughtful deep down.

-Deep-deep-down.

During the pass-the-parcel game -in my honour, I was given all sorts of thoughtful gifts for my baby. Enough baby-grows and bibs to clothe an entire army of little babies, plus some bizarre contraption designed to milk me, apparently! Steph offered to help me get to grips with it, but to her disappointment I politely declined.

Carly's game of pass-up-on-the-package was equally as generous. She now had enough knickers and negligees to keep a brothel happy.

All-in-all, we had quite a fun time. Although, I must admit I thought Steph had gone a step to far with the cake. A pink penis cake was one thing, but handing Carly a knife and asking her to cut the cake I thought was a little insensitive.

"Hey," Steph chided me when I tutted at it, "did you see that video on YouTube that she made me watch? This is payback for her traumatising me!"

Ouch!

***

A couple of hours later and all of the guests had gone. I sat on the sofa between Carly and Steph, musing over how much my life had changed in the last year.

"You know, don't take this the wrong way Claire, but you're much more fun then you used to be." Steph said, picking sparkly confetti out of her drink.

"Thank you. I think!"

"No I mean it, you used to be so quiet and timid. I much prefer you now."

"What, now I've had a nervous breakdown and

lost the plot?" I smiled.

"No. Well, yeah, I suppose. I don't know, you just seemed to have come out of your shell a lot more lately. It's good. A definite improvement."

"Thanks."

"I still think your taste in men is shit though." She added with a sigh.

"Noted!"

"I thought you and Colin would get on."

"You mean the one with the nose hair from the speed dating?"

"Hey with a bit of primping he could've been alright."

"A bit of primping? He needed a hedge trimmer taking to his face! Honestly, I couldn't take my eyes off his nostrils!"

Steph waved me away. "It wasn't that noticeable."

"It quivered when he talked!"

She pulled a face at me.

Carly yawned into her 'Penis Collider' as Steph called it. "I don't mind Max quite so much lately. He seems a lot more...normal than before. He seems...happier."

I nodded. "He is, he's like the man I married again. The one I fell in love with at fifteen."

Steph asked, "So you've been together that long?"

"Yep."

"What was he like back then?"

I blushed a little. "He was alright."

"Ah come on?" Carly hit me over the head with a cushion. "Give us more than that?"

"Okay, okay." I laughed rubbing my head. "He was a bad boy. At fifteen he was already well off the rails. He rode a stolen motorbike and smoked twenty a day."

"Never!" they burst out together.

"Oh yeah. To my little fifteen-year-old brain he was like James Dean."

"Ugh!" Steph exclaimed wrinkling up her nose.

"So what happened?" Carly asked.

"I don't know. Life I suppose. We all have to grow up sometimes."

"Not me." Steph said decidedly. "I fully intend to grow old disgracefully."

I looked down at the cup in my hand shaped like a woman's breast before replying, "I believe you."

I put the cup on the coffee table in front of me before staggering to my feet. "Right ladies, that's me done I'm afraid. Time to make tracks."

I was almost to the front door when the doorbell rang.

"Get that will you on your way out Claire?" Called Steph from the kitchen.

"Righto."

I pulled the door open to find a familiar looking man in a suit. "Hello?" I asked him curiously.

"Good evening madam. Could I interest you in any double glaz.....Oh? Oh dear!"

He took a step away from me in horror, clutching his briefcase against his chest. "Oh dear! Oh dear, oh dear!"

"Hey," I said, "I remember you!"

"Pardon me madam, I'll be off now." He turned away hurriedly.

"Wait! Come back!" I set off after him.

"Please stop chasing me!" He called from the stairs below me. "I'm really very sorry."

"Wait! Come back! I have to apologise to you!"

He carried on hurrying down the stairs two at a time. "Nothing to apologise for, it's quite alright!"

"Will you bloody stop!" I called breathlessly.

"No!"

I was starting to get quite cross. Damn this bloody bump; it made it so difficult to run. I peered down the stairwell after him. At this rate I'd never catch him to apologise. I slid off one of my trainers and took aim at his head carefully, one, two, three.... pop! Got him!

Once he was laid out on the landing below, I managed to catch up to him. By the time I got to him I was breathless and had to sit down on the step next to him whilst he was sitting on the floor rubbing his head.

He looked up at me startled. "What did you do that for?"

"I needed you to stop so that I could apologise to you."

"It's okay," he said, still rubbing his head, "happens all the time."

"What, mad women kicking you and throwing shoes at you?"

"Well, no, but I have been punched once or twice. Although no one but you ever tried to sell me a suit that came with a complimentary pube."

"Oh. You caught me on an off day, and I'm…I'm really very sorry that I attacked you."

He looked at me warily. "Okay. Thank you?"

"And the pube wasn't mine." I had to make that clear.

He raised an eyebrow at me before letting me help him to his feet and dusting off his jacket. "Right then, I'll be off."

"Okay. Once again, I really am sorry."

"All in a day's work." He called over his shoulder as he hurried off quickly.

I heard a noise above me and looked up to see Carly and Steph grinning down at me over the bannister. Steph called down, "Are you causing trouble again?"

I shook my head. "No, just repairing a bit of damage."

The salesman was still rubbing his head and staring at me as he got to his feet, he didn't seem to want to turn his back to me one bit.

"Look," I said, "I'm moving into a new house soon, and guess what? It doesn't have double glazing! Why don't you give me your card or something and you can pop round and give me a quote?"

He shook his head at me slowly. "Is this a trick?"

"No. I genuinely need double glazing."

"And you don't want me to buy anything...."

"No, I just want windows...and a door." I added with an excited nod.

He narrowed his eyes at me for a moment before sliding his hand into his breast pocket and retrieving a business card. Without taking his eyes off mine he slowly rested his card on the ground between us before backing off slowly.

"Thanks." I said as I bent to retrieve it. I obviously startled him as he then set off running down the stairs two at a time. "I'll call you then!" I yelled after him.

I heard the door downstairs slam behind him.

Chapter - Thirty - Six

"So what do you think?" Max asked me with a grin as he carried me over the threshold of our new home.

"I think it's shit!" Paul sulked from behind us. "It's too far away from Jenny and my mates."

Max and I shook our heads at each other in despair.

"Just two more years and he'll be at Uni." Max announced for the tenth time that day. It had become like a mantra to us lately. We were literally counting the days!

"I love it." I told Max as he sat me gently on my feet.

"Oo, mind ya back." He pulled me out of the way as a removal man staggered through the doorway behind us with the first of the boxes. "I better help." He said with a sigh taking his jacket off.

There wasn't much I could do to help -with my being so far gone now. I was two weeks away from my due date and praying for the day to arrive. Paul could have helped -but he was a teenage arsehole. He'd had a big hoo-ha that morning when he couldn't find the right shade black eyeliner because I'd had the nerve to pack his 'product' box (make-up bag.) And, God forbid he should chip one of his perfectly manicured-black fingernails on a box. I stared at him appraisingly for a minute before grabbing him by the sleeve. "Come with me."

"What? Get off, you'll stretch my top!" He whined.

I ignored his protests and dragged him along behind me back through the front door.

"Where are we going you demented Umpalumpa?" (His pet name for his poor pregnant mother, with only a slightly bad spray tan.)

"We're going to give a nice old lady a laugh."

"Get off!"

I ignored him as I wove us past the removal men and off down the street towards Violet's House.

I knocked softly on her front window while TLS whinged and shrugged himself free from my grip with a scowl.

"Goodness me!" Violet declared as she opened her front door and came face to face with Paul. She briefly glanced at me with a worried smile, before returning her stare at my son's grumpy head.

"Hi Violet," I offered, "I just moved in opposite, and thought I'd pop across and apologise for my behaviour the last time I saw you. I was a bit out of sorts and said a lot of stupid things. Anyway, sorry for that."

She shook her head a little bemused I think.

"That's okay, I took it something must have upset you a great deal." She returned a puzzled look at Paul.

"Oh sorry, this is my son Paul. I believe I once tried to describe his hair to you, well I thought a picture paints a thousand words so I've brought him for you to have a giggle at."

I swear Paul would've kicked me if he could've done, the fury on his face was priceless.

"Well you'd better both come in then." Violet said holding the door open with an amused glint in her eye.

"Take you shoes off." I ordered Paul.

With a huff he sat on the floor to start unlacing his Dr Martins. I felt a smirk start on my face as he toddled off behind Violet in his Teenage-mutant-ninja-turtle socks.

"Well it's very nice to see you again my dear." Violet said after pouring me a cup of tea. "Now, would you like some pop sweetheart?" She asked Paul as though she was speaking to a toddler.

Oh he was going to kill me for this; I bit the smirk from my lips.

"I'll just have tea, ta." He replied through gritted teeth.

She pulled a packet of jammy dodgers from out of her apron pocket and cut them open with a pair of scissors before emptying them on a plate in front of us. "Dig in." She ordered.

"So you really do have horns." She said as she sat

down and put her glasses on for a closer look. Paul looked terrified as she began peering closer at his head. "However do you get your hair to stay up like that? Doesn't the rest of your head get cold love?" She paused thoughtfully, "I expect you can't get close to your dad when he's hedge trimming eh?"

Paul glared at me over his shaking cup of tea.

I almost choked on my tea. I looked up to see Violet examining Paul closely, fascinated I think. Once her evaluation of my son was over she sat back in her chair to drink her own tea, though still obviously fascinated by him. Paul was eyeing her warily from the far side of the sofa. I looked at Violet and Paul for a moment before it dawned on me that they were probably going through the same phase, all be it at different stages of their lives. I looked from Paul -with his horns and eyeliner, to the little old lady with the purple rinse and crazy eyeshadow. Yep they definitely had something in common. I would have to tell Paul when we got home how alike he and Violet were, he'd like that I'm sure.

"So you're not Jewish anymore then?" Violet asked me.

"Erm, no." I felt myself flush a little.

"Oh, so you know about her being Jewish then?" Paul asked, suddenly animated at the thought of embarrassing me.

"Oh yes, I know about the menorah, and the.... Bah mitzvah." She looked down, suddenly fascinated by her slippers.

Oh God, I told her about giving the Jewish boy condoms didn't I? Shit!

"All just a big misunderstanding Violet." I fluffed.

"Oh yes," TLS joined in with a smirk, "but it's not every guest turns up at a boy's thirteenth birthday party armed with cherry-flavoured condoms is it though Mum?"

I'll kill him for this.

He was obviously waiting for an answer, the smug little git.

"Your condoms though Paul, not mine." I returned, sipping my tea.

"That's obvious by the state of *you* isn't it. If you'd *kept* the condoms instead of offending the entire local Jewish community with them, you might not be in *that* state!"

"How dare you!"

"Well it wasn't planned was it!" He spat.

I was horrified. "I am so sorry Violet. Paul, say sorry to Violet."

"What for, *she's* not pregnant."

I took a breath in sharply, shocked to my core that he could be so rude in front of Violet. Before I knew what I was doing I was on my feet with Violet's scissors in one hand and Paul's left horn in the other -and with one swift chop it was no-longer attached to his head.

He stared at me open-mouthed as I held his

horn before his shocked eyes. He rubbed his stump in disbelief that his beloved horn had gone. It was at that point that I felt a wave of hysteria threatening to break out. Though I was horrified at what I had done, and how quickly I had done it without even thinking, all I could see was Paul with a single horn sticking out of his head like a wonky unicorn. I swear it's one of the funniest things I've ever seen. He looked like a heavy-duty Alf-Alpha.

His face was puce as I put down Violet's scissors carefully back on the biscuit tray where I'd found them. I zipped my hoody up over my bump and up to my neck before sticking my chin in the air and thanking Violet for a lovely tea, but we'd have to be leaving now. We had unpacking to do.

"That's okay lovey," she replied, 'it was nice to... erm. Well it was...well, I'll see you soon I expect, now you're living over the road." She said the last part with a slight grimace, I swear. Oh well, I was a dab hand at alienating my neighbours now anyway. I might as well start as I mean to go on.

"Come on you!" I ordered Paul, who was struggling to do up his laces whilst clasping the remains of his hair firmly in one hand. "I'll glue it back on or something when we get home." I crossed my fingers behind my back.

He glared at me, got to his feet and stomped off up the road to our new house without a backward glance at me, single horn bobbing on the side of his head in the breeze.

I turned back to Violet who was still standing in the doorway. "I'm so sorry about that Violet, I don't know what came over me."

"That's alright. He's quite a handful isn't he."

"That's putting it mildly. I shouldn't have done what I did though. He *was* right, my baby wasn't planned, but he had no right to be so rude to me."

"That's kids though isn't it." She said sagely. "He'll soon grow out of it."

"I'd pray for it, but I don't believe."

Chapter - Thirty - Seven

I could hear the laughter coming from my new house before I even opened the front door. Max was doubled-up laughing as Paul was thrusting up his shorn locks in the air in rage at what I had dared do to him. The madder Paul got -the more Max was in hysterics.

"Go on, keep nodding your head Paul." He ordered before laughing again at the single horn wobble.

"It's not funny!" Paul stamped his foot in temper. "I look retarded!"

"You *are* retarded," Max retorted, "you'd have to be to make yourself look that stupid. It's time you grew-up and stopped playing dress-up with your little friends. They've already warned you that you'll get expelled from sixth-form if you look like that. There's more important things in life than stupid hair and eyeliner!"

"I don't remember you ever saying that to mum when *she's* got stupid hair and eyeliner."

"Your mother can have her stupid hair anyway she damn-well pleases."

Ouch! What the hell do they mean? Do I have

stupid hair? Oh no, not something else to worry about! I twiddled with a loose strand of it self-consciously as I watched them from the doorway.

TLS dove into one of the cardboard boxes that Max had thoughtfully written *'TLS's shit!'* on with felt tip pen. After rummaging around in there for a while he came back up for air with a black woolly-hat clamped firmly on his head -though it bulged quite a lot on one side, it did make him look less funny. He barged past me whilst looking pointedly in the other direction.

"Where are you going?" I yelled after him.

"Where do you think? Bloody hairdressers, see if they can fix it."

"Good luck with that!" I sighed, as I closed the front door behind him.

Max shook his head at me with a smirk. "What did you do." It wasn't a question.

"I snapped and before I knew it I had scissors in one hand and his hair in the other."

"Well it was bound to happen wasn't it. If you didn't do it, I was going to swap his shampoo for immac anyway." He shrugged with a smile and got back on moving boxes.

Oh well, so much for a nice calm moving-in day!

***

Apart from the awful start to moving day, the rest of the day was nice and calm. The house we were moving into had been fully renovated before we moved in -apart from double glazing, and so all we had to do was plonk our furniture down and put a few pairs of curtains and blinds up here and there. It was the easiest move we've ever undertaken.

I had mentioned the subject of double-glazing to Max earlier and told him about wanting to make amends with the double-glazing sales-man, but unbeknownst to me, we weren't allowed double-glazing due to it being a 'heritage area', any changes to the façade would need permission from the council. Whoops! Perhaps it's a good thing that the salesman scarpered before I could give him my address to call at. Imagine my embarrassment if I had to turn him away a second time, after I had *invited* him!

I wandered around my new home, room to room admiring the lovely period features that I had never had before, stained-glass-window on the stairs, I noted smugly; cornice in every room, par-quet floor in my hallway, and best of all, a proper chandelier in the living room. Not a tacky repro thing, but the real McCoy, proper antique brass and crystal. I beamed inwardly. I loved the place already. I hovered in what would be our nursery. It was currently painted out a soft lemon colour, but what colour would it be next? Pink, or blue? I wish I'd had the nerve to ask the sex. Max thinks I'm stupid for not wanting to know. He doesn't understand, I *do* want to know, but I want to *know* that it's a girl. Oh God that makes me sound awful doesn't it. I'll still love it if it's a boy, it's just that the thought of another boy like Paul scares the crap out of me. Girls *have* to be easier, don't they? I know I'm not the best parent in the world, or probably even in this street, but please don't let me screw it up this time!

Later on that night, Max and I were in the middle of cooking our supper when TLS burst through the front door with a bang and headed straight past us, hat still firmly jammed on his head -though no-longer bulging at one side I noted.

"How did you get on at the hairdressers?" Max asked through a mouthful of pudding.

"Alright," he grunted. "I'm just getting changed and going out."

"Where are you going?" I asked in surprise. He seemed in a suspiciously good mood compared to earlier.

"Met a bird in the hairdressers. I'm taking her to the pictures in an hour."

"What? What about Jenny?" I asked bewildered.

"Ah, she lives too far away. I can't afford a woman that far away. Bus fares are ridiculous!"

"So who's the new woman?" Max asked smirking.

"Paula something-or-other. She's well fit. Luckily for me she likes skin-heads."

I gasped in horror as he whipped his hat off to reveal a shiny pink pin-head. "What have you done?"

He shook his head agreeably. "Well I was all set just to have the other horn cut off and just have it tidied up, maybe have a stripe put in it, but then Paula talked me into the skin look. I haven't seen it yet but it feels awesome."

"Why haven't you seen it? Hairdressers always show you a mirror."

"Yeah but Paula said hers was broken."

I was getting a sinking feeling. "Please tell me Paula isn't the hairdresser?"

"I told you, I met her at the hairdressers. D'oh, 'course it's going to be a hairdresser, it's a gent's barbershop and I am defo not into dudes."

"How old is she?" I panicked.

"I don't know, thirty maybe?"

"What?" W.T.F?

Max grabbed me calmly by the elbow. "Just leave it for now."

"But...."

He shook his head. "Trust me."

Paul looked at the pair of us as if we'd grown an extra nipple or something before departing up the stairs with a –"Laters!"

"But..." I started again.

Max shook his head again. "Just wait."

We each looked at the ceiling as Paul went thundering across it upstairs towards the bathroom. We heard his yelp as he saw his reflection in the mirror for the first time.

Max grinned, "I don't think he's going to like Paula quite so much now he's seen what she's done to him. No wonder she wouldn't give him a mirror, he looks terrible!"

"What possessed him?" I wondered aloud. "He knows he has an egg-shaped head, how on earth could he think making it egg coloured would be a good look?"

"Beats me."

"At least he can't get thrown out of sixth-form now." I muttered. "If they have a problem with his new look we'll just have to say the stress of starting college and moving house has given him alopecia!"

"Just as long as your mum doesn't get hold of him." Max yawned. "If she starts spouting all her racist bullshit at him he might come home with a bloody swastika tattoo!"

"Over my dead body. If he gets any tattoo it'd better be an 'I love Mum' one."

"I wouldn't get your hopes up."

Chapter-Thirty-Eight

"So Claire," my imposter therapist said with glee, "this is your last session I believe?"

"Yes, thank goodness." I fiddled in my seat as I couldn't get comfortable on little chairs anymore due to the size of my big-fat-pregnant arse.

"And how are *we* feeling today?"

"Well *I* am feeling shit; I don't know about you."

"Oo tetchy today aren't *we*?"

"*I'm* not, why are you?" What is this 'we' business about? I'm not a toddler.

She stared at me for what seemed like an age. God these people are so infuriating.

Finally, she spoke. "Is this tetchiness down to the pregnancy or is there any other issues that you wish to talk about?"

"Well look at me," I said, "I'm the size of a whale, and I'm about to drop any minute. I've got a baby sitting on my bladder, the little bugger is all elbows and knees and I swear to god it's actually biting me in there."

She smiled smugly at me, shaking her head. "I don't think a baby *can* bite, they don't have teeth."

"Old people don't have teeth either but it doesn't

stop 'em devouring pork chops!"

She pretty much ignored everything I was telling her with a wave of her hand. "So am I right in thinking that your crankiness is simply pregnancy related?"

I took a deep breath before conceding that perhaps she may have a point. "I just don't remember feeling this bad the first time around. I'm hoping that because it seems to be different this time it might be because I'm having a girl."

"Claire, you have to be prepared that you may well be having a boy. Wishful thinking doesn't change the facts. You have a fifty/fifty chance of having a girl. That's not good odds to be betting on by anyone's standards."

"I know, I'm just *sure* that it's a girl."

"But what if it's not?"

"If it's not a girl, I'll still love it. I'll just know that it's going to be harder rearing a boy again."

"Why do you insist on this theory of yours that girls are somehow easier? From my own personal experience, I would have to disagree with you."

I sat forward a little as she had now caught my attention. "How so?"

She looked thoughtful for a moment. "Well, I have one son and three daughters and my son is without a doubt the easiest of the bunch. I've never had a bit of trouble from him but by God those girls of mine could put me in an early grave. If it's not bad boyfriends or pregnancy scares, it's PMT or getting arrested for stealing make-up from Superdrug. Trust me, if you *do* have a boy, count your blessings."

I found myself rubbing my bump softly whilst I pondered this new angle. I hadn't thought about the downside to having a girl. My sister had tried to warn me but I hadn't taken much heed of her, I had been too preoccupied with thoughts of shopping trips and trying on each other clothes. I hadn't given a thought to chasing her boyfriend out of her bedroom window in the middle of the night with a sweeping brush aimed at his genitals.

She interrupted me from my thoughts. "Is there anything else you wish to talk about today? This is, after all, your last session so if there is anything else that you'd like to get off your chest, now's the time."

I thought about it. "Other than my normal issues, I think I'm good."

She nodded. "I think so too. In the last few sessions alone I've seen an improvement. You seem perfectly able to voice your frustrations now without bottling them up until it becomes something you have no control over."

"Yeah, I have to agree, although I'm grumpy all of the time though."

"Grumpy is good, it's healthy and it's honest. There's nothing worse than pasting a false smile on your face and pretending everything's fine when it isn't."

"Yeah, I've found that." I shuffled in my chair a little trying to get more comfortable. I had terrible back ache. "My mother called yesterday to inform me that I would have to have the baby christened or she would cut me out of the will. So I told her that she could stick her will up her bum for all I care, my baby is going to be a Godless heathen and proud."

She smiled at me, I think for some reason she finds me amusing. She's certainly an improvement on my last therapist -although I'm starting to wonder if she was a real therapist or just a patient with identity issues that had wandered into my therapy room. She certainly hadn't seemed very.... balanced. I winced for a moment as another wave of indigestion caught me off guard.

"Are you alright Claire?" she asked looking a little concerned at me.

I paused for a moment to get my breath back. "I'm alright, I just keep getting awful indigestion." This was getting worse and worse by the minute. Actually if I didn't know better I could almost think this was...oh.

I slowly got to my feet as I felt my waters break. Ugh! I looked in horror at my therapist who had suddenly gone white as a sheet, holding her hands over her mouth in shock. As she traced her eyes around the puddle at my feet she began pulling her holdall away from the wet patch beneath my chair.

"I am so sorry..." I began before a wave of pain hit me, knocking me back into my seat.

She made a run for the door to fetch Max from the waiting room outside. With my due-date being tomorrow, Max had insisted on staying by my side 'just-in-case,' a wise move in retrospect.

He burst through the door a moment later looking both terrified and excited. "Come on then!" He exclaimed.

Chapter Thirty-Nine

"Excuse me." I whispered. "Excuse me please, can you just..." I trailed off as another nurse ignored me and swept past my bed without making eye contact. It was the middle of the night and I had just woken up after giving birth earlier in the evening. I don't remember much about what happened during the birth other than losing a lot of blood and having to have emergency transfusions. The pain had been much worse than I remembered it being when I had Paul, I thought second time around would be easier. But apparently not!

I had pieced together what had happened to me so far from the cleaner that had been busy bleaching the floor beneath my bed when I came around. Max was nowhere to be seen and no nurses seemed able to see me. At least Brenda the night-cleaner on my ward seemed more helpful.

"By you had a rough ride lass." She told me with a shake of her head and a flip of her mop. "By the time the baby came you were delirious. You took one look at the little mite and passed out. You'd had it bad though, I could hear you crying out from the corridor."

I rubbed my head. "I don't remember it coming out. Where is it, and where's my husband?"

She carried on scrubbing as she talked. "The baby'll be here soon I expect. They've probably took if off for a feed while you were asleep. As for that fella of yours, he'll be home in bed. Visiting ends at 9pm. They're ever so strict about visitors on this ward."

"Oh." I felt very dejected. This wasn't how I imagined it to be one bit. Where's my husband with the giant inappropriate teddy in one hand and a big bouquet of roses in the other? Why have I only got Brenda the cleaner with a mop in one hand and Dettol in the other?

"Right then, I'll be off now sweetie." She said with a wave of her marigold glove.

"Bye then." I called after her.

I carefully pulled myself up a little into more of a sitting position and peered around me, through the dim night-lights I could see another three beds in the room that all seemed to contain sleeping women. One to my left and two to my right. After staring at the ceiling for a while I found the soft snores from the women around me seemed to lull me back off to sleep. I fought tiredness for a while as I wanted to be awake to see my baby when they brought it back, but I had to admit defeat and let my eyelids close.

***

It was the sound of a baby crying that eventually woke me up a few hours later. I turned my head to the right and squinted as I noticed the crib that had been placed by the side of my bed as I'd slept. Instantly awake with excitement now, I opened my eyes wide with delight as I saw my baby wrapped up in a pink blanket! A Pink blanket! Pink! It's a girl!

"Oh!" I exclaimed loudly, "It's a girl!"

"It sure is." Said the petite dark haired girl in the next bed. "Isn't she beautiful."

"Oh she's the most beautiful thing I've ever seen!" I was pulling myself up and straining my neck to see her better as all I could see at the moment was the pink blanket. "Let's have a look at you then." I cooed as I reached my hand over and pulled back the pink blanket. "What the...?" I leaped back in shock at the little black baby girl gurgling up at me adoringly. "What?" I scratched my head baffled. "This isn't mine." I told the girl in the next bed.

"I know." She said, looking at me strangely. "She's mine." Then helpfully she informed me: - "Yours is over there."

"Oh. Thank you." I turned to my left and saw another glass crib parked next to the other side of my bed. I peered over the edge of my bed warily. "Oh, hello there." I told the little bundle of blue blankets before adding, "Blue's a funny colour to dress a girl in isn't it." I pulled myself further over to the other side of the bed so that I could reach the crib easier. I reached a hand out and gently pulled the crib further towards me. I peered down into the blankets and my heart melted at the little scrap of a thing laid there asleep. "Hi." I gushed down at him. "Oh you're so beautiful. My little sweetheart!"

"Are you ready to hold him?" A nurse asked smiling as she came over to my bed.

"Yes please."

She gently picked him up and placed him in my waiting arms. I don't know if I was laughing or crying as I held him -as if for dear life.

"My little boy."

***

"So what are you going to call it?" TLS demanded later when Max dragged him in for a visit.

I looked at Max who shrugged back at me. Max had named Paul, and now it was my turn to name our second son. I had an idea for a name, but it was a bit radical so I wished to keep it to myself for as long as possible in the hope that no-one could talk me out of it before I had chance to register his birth and get that name on the birth certificate.

I shrugged back at Paul. "Not sure yet, I'm still thinking."

"Do you want to hold your baby brother?" Max asked him as he cradled the little one.

TLS peered over before sniffing at the baby and declaring, "Nope, it stinks."

Max and I exchanged an exasperated shake of our

heads.

"Just two more years to go remember." Max consoled me.

"It's just not bloody quick enough though is it." I rubbed my head with self-pity as I looked at the grumpy bald teenager glaring at me from across the bed.

"I *am* here you know!" He chided. "I do have ears!"

"And *I* can see them now you're bald." Max said as he flicked one of Paul's ear lobes cheekily.

"OW!"

"Has anyone heard from Carly yet?" I had been just as worried for Carly coming into hospital yesterday as I was for myself. I couldn't believe that I wasn't there to see her before she went to theatre. I had supposed to meet her at the hospital after my last therapy session, but you know how that ended.

"She's fine, she's awake but groggy." Max answered. "As far as they can tell everything went according to plan. It's just going to be a long recovery."

"When can I see her?"

"I've asked if you can stop in for a few minutes this evening before I take you home. They said that's fine as long as you don't stay too long. Obviously she's exhausted and on a lot of pain relief."

"I can't wait to see her."

***

"Carly!" I hissed quietly at the sleeping figure in the bed. "Carly!" I hadn't recognised her at first and had inadvertently walked past her bed a few times before I noticed her name on the white-board behind her. I'd never seen her without her wig and full black-up make-up. There's no wonder I didn't recognise the bald, white figure laid in the bed. I assume they'd made her scrub off the make-up for theatre.

"Hey?" I whispered softly as she opened her eyes. "How you feeling?"

"Shit." She said groggily.

"Understandable."

She looked down at my belly for a moment before the penny dropped. "You've had the baby?"

"Yes, last night. I was gonna bring it in to show you but they wouldn't let me, no babies allowed."

"Bummer. So what did you have? What is it?"

"It's a boy!" I said laughing.

"Aw, one of each then." Carly grinned before pulling her sheet back and declaring, "Because it's a girl!"

Chapter Forty

"I can't keep calling him little man." Max complained a few days later. "Can't you just make up your mind and name him already." He was walking up and down our living room rocking our son gently to try and get him to stop crying.

"I've got an appointment to register him tomorrow at 11 o clock. I have to have a name by then so don't worry."

"But I *am* worried. I want the chance to at least *veto* a name if you try and name him something stupid."

"I won't name him anything stupid I promise. He's going to have a cool name, something other kids'll envy." I looked away sharply. Oh God I hope the other kids will envy his name and not pick on him for it.

We were interrupted from our bickering by the sound of the letterbox banging.

"Post!" I announced getting slowly to my feet and shuffling off to collect the mail from off the doormat. I was quite glad to put an end to the 'name' conversation. If I wasn't careful Max would end up wheedling it out of me. It was my turn to pick a name and by God I had picked a name!

I bent down and picked a postcard up from off the doormat. It showed a picture of Buddha I think. Some fat-cross-legged statue anyway. I flipped it over to try and decipher the scruffy hand-writing on the back. For a start someone had sent it to our old house. Good job we'd had our mail re-directed. Once my eyes got a handle on the childish scrawl I began to read.

Dear Claire,
I just wanted to say thank you to you for changing my life. If you and your pube in the jam tart hadn't caused me to question my entire existence I would probably still be stuck listening to people like you whining on in therapy all day-everyday, depressing the crap out of me. Instead, I'm now back-packing my way around the world and loving every minute of my life, so Claire, thank you.
All my best
Madeline (Your poor frazzled ex-therapist)

I grinned to myself, I told her it would all come right in the end. With a whistle I ambled back through to the living room to lay down and watch Max wearing out the new carpet trying to get our baby boy to sleep.

"I'm not going to change the conversation." Max whispered softly. "I want to know the name."

Shit. I decided I better lie. "When I know,

you'll know."

"I can't come with you tomorrow to register the birth, I've got that meeting in Manchester and I really can't get out of it."

I knew, that was why I picked this particular time slot. "It's okay, my sister said she'll drive me."

"Oh, good." He paused for a moment. "On the subject of driving, you really are going to have to get your license back you know. I've been making enquiries about it. You'll have to do a re-test but it shouldn't take you too long to pick it back up."

What? Hell no. My driving days are well over.

I was spared the oncoming argument by TLS who burst into the room and dropped a folder down on the sofa next to me. "What's this?" I queried.

"Homework, but I don't have time to do it. I figured since you chopped my hair off -and just sat and did nothing after that bitch-hairdresser scalped me, you owe me. So here it is, I'm calling in the favour."

"Oh you are -are you!" The cheeky little sod. I picked the folder up and flipped it open. "What's it about? What's it for?"

"It's for English, it's about the butterfly effect theory. You know like in that film, where the little things you do in life end up having massive consequences later on. Shit like that, you know."

Oh I think I did!

As he stomped off back to his room I pulled

out a pen and changed his title from 'The Butterfly Effect' to 'The Pube in the Jam Tart Effect'. Yes, I think I could work with this, I grinned.

***

"Okay, here goes." I told Rachel as I filled in the form to saddle my child for life with my name of choice. I could see her straining over my shoulder to see what I was writing. I blocked her from viewing with a smirk before handing the form across to the registrar.

She whined, "Come on you're killing me here, what are you calling him?"

The registrar looked down at the form and smirked at Rachel and then looked away as she carried on typing.

"I am calling him -because of the circumstances that led to his existence..."

"Not Jam tart! You can't call my nephew Jam tart!"

"I'm not calling him Jam tart, stupid. I'm calling him -in honour of the jam tart- *Kipling*."

"You can't call him Kipling!"

"I can, it's cool, it's different."

"It's a frigging cake. The poor bugger's going to go through his entire life being called Mr Kipling."

"But what a conversation starter his name will be."

After fiddling with her phone for a few minutes she cried out. "Do you know what the name Kipling actually means?"

"Well I assume it's something to do with cakes?"

"Nope. According to google, the definition of Kipling is '*cured salmon.*' This just gets worse by the minute." She shook her head at me in despair as the registrar handed me the birth certificate. "Come on," she ordered, "Let's go break the news to Max."

As we were heading back to her car I was following a few steps behind her -as I can never keep up with my fast-paced sister, when she turned around suddenly blocking my path. "Wait right there." She ordered.

"What? What's wrong?"

"You picked a middle name as well, I saw you fill out that extra box. Come on, out with it. We agreed if you had a cool first name you were going to give him a hideous middle name on badness. Well, since you seem to consider Kipling as a cool name, that must mean you did something awful for the middle name."

"Actually I did something ace for his middle name. It was Mum actually who inspired it."

"So, you didn't give him a stupid girly middle name? Thank God, 'cause that poor kid's gonna have enough to worry about."

"Here." I said, handing over the birth certificate. "See for yourself."

She snatched it from me and tore open the envelope. After unfolding the piece of paper she did a double-take and took a sharp breath in. I smiled smugly, yes the name might be a little shocking but it's definitely cool.

"You didn't!" She whispered.

"I bloody did." I grinned.

"But I was only joking about the middle name thing."

"Come on it's not that bad, I think it's cool. Like I say, it was Mum that inspired it calling my baby a godless heathen. Well I thought why not embrace it. *Kipling Heathen Porter*. I think it's got quite a ring to it, don't you?"

She turned the certificate around me to see. "You didn't name him Kipling Heathen; you've named him Kipling Heather. The poor little bugger has a girl's name for a middle name!"

I felt my heart sink into my knees as I snatched the birth certificate up to see for myself. I nearly fainted as I saw *Kipling Heather Porter.* "But that's not what I wrote." I insisted.

"It's your crap handwriting that is." She offered helpfully. "She's thought your N was an R. Easy mistake really."

"Noooo!" I fell against her car as my legs gave way. "Max's gonna kill me!"

She was laughing now. "On the plus side, like you said, his name is a hell of a conversation starter."

I sniffed as I got in the passenger seat. "There's always deed poll isn't there."

She shook her head and laughed at me.

The End

Acknowledgements

This book would not be possible without help from the following people:- Tom and Sophia Smith for their tireless help and production of the book cover, my amazing parents Chris and Steve Lines for their endless love and support and for encouraging my -sometimes irresponsible - sense of humour, my wonderful parents-in-law Ken and Marny Smith for caring and looking out for me, my brilliant brother-in-law Kevin Smith for all his help and support, and finally, my loving late-husband Shaun who loved this book and gave me the greatest compliment by laughing all the way through it.

Also by K.L. Smith

Flight of the Cuckoo

Cuckoo's Nest

Just a little Cuckoo – Coming Soon

The Little Pink Pill

Hello

Merlstead Heights Hotel

The P**e in the Jam Tart

Printed in Great Britain
by Amazon